Music:

The Keynote of Human Evolution

*This is the first volume
in a series of three
bearing the inclusive title*
MUSIC — IT'S POWER AND MAGIC

VOL. I
MUSIC — THE KEYNOTE OF HUMAN EVOLUTION

VOL. II
THE COSMIC HARP

VOL. III
BEETHOVEN'S NINE SYMPHONIES
Correlated with the
NINE SPIRITUAL MYSTERIES

SAINT CECELIA

FROM A DESIGN BY F. S. CHURCH

Music:
The Keynote of Human Evolution

By CORINNE HELINE

NEW AGE BIBLE & PHILOSOPHY CENTER
1139 Lincoln Blvd.
Santa Monica, CA 90403

REPRINTED 1986

NEW AGE WRITINGS BY CORINNE HELINE

New Age Bible Interpretation

Old Testament
> Vol I - Five Books of Moses and Joshua
> Vol II - Part I. Solomon and the Temple Builders
> Part II. Books of Initiation
> Vol III - Part I. The Promise
> Part II. The Preparation

New Testament
> Vol IV. Preparation for coming of the Light of the World
> Vol V. The Christ and His Mission
> Vol VI. The Work of the Apostles and Paul and Book of Revelation
> Vol VII Mystery of the Christos

Other Books on Bible Interpretation

Tarot and the Bible - Mythology and the Bible - Mystic Masonry and the Bible - Occult Anatomy and the Bible - The Bible and the Stars - Sacred Science of Numbers - Questions and Answers on Bible Enigmas - Easter Mysteries - Christmas Mysteries - Supreme Initiations of the Blessed Virgin.

Other Works

Magic Gardens - Star Gates - Color and Music in the New Age - Music: the Keynote of Human Evolution - The Cosmic Harp - Healing and Regeneration through Color - Healing and Regeneration through Music - Esoteric Music of Richard Wagner - Beethoven's Nine Symphonies - The Twelve Labors of Hercules - Mysteries of the Holy Grail

NEW AGE WRITINGS BY THEODORE HELINE

America's Destiny, The American Indian, The Archetype Unveiled - Capital Punishment - Esoteric Drama Studies - Romeo and Juliet - The Merchant of Venice - Saint Francis and the Wolf of Gubbio

•••

A current price list may be obtained from

New Age Bible and Philosophy Center
1139 Lincoln Boulevard
Santa Monica, California 90403

Telephone (?13) 395-4346

This volume is dedicated to ST. CECE
whose highly inspirational life made
a perfect instrument for the reception
transmission of the supreme art of Mu
Also to all New Age disciples of
sublime art whose aspiration is to se
this highest of arts at a correspo
lofty level.

Music Is the Universal Language
God is its center;
infinity its circumference.

INTRODUCTION

IN ACCORDANCE with the rapid tempo of our modern age, the general public is accustomed to the fact that music is being seriously considered as a healing factor by accredited practitioners representative of various methods endorsed by the healing profession. Some of the more progressive hospitals are engaging musicians as full-time members of their regular staff. This intensely interesting expansion of the art of music in relation to constructive usage is entirely in keeping with developments preparing for the coming Aquarian Air Age, and has long been predicted by occult scientists. The current atomic era heralds an amazing advance in music as a healing medium.

The most successful practitioners of the New Age will consider man's invisible vehicles together with his physical body as making up a complete unit, for it is upon the inner or finer vehicles that musical therapy produces its most potent effects. Paracelsus, the noted occult physician of the sixteenth century, stated: "The true healer looks not for causes in the visible but seeks to understand the invisible."

All life is a vibration. Differentiation is due to the one Divine Life vibrating at varying rates. Hence, vibration is the key to the secret of both health and sickness, youth and old age, death and its ultimate surrender to immortality. The fundamental condition underlying man's well-being is *harmony*. In obedience to the Law of Harmony, man was made "in the image and likeness of God." Had he continued to function in attunement with that law, physical imperfections and diseases would have been unknown to him.

Trends of the New Day point to man's acceptance of this universal truth along with an inner realization that

[ix]

it is within his own divine power to recreate, here and now, conditions in accordance with the initial pattern. One of the noblest of all arts, music, is in the vanguard of this most glorious work: *the perfection of man by means of reawakening the divinity within himself.*

TABLE OF CONTENTS

Contents

Chapter I

MUSIC IN RELATION TO HUMAN EVOLUTION

COSMIC MUSIC

Music is the harmonious voice of creation; an echo of the invisible world, one note of the divine concord which the entire universe is destined one day to sound.—*Mazzini*

Ah, music, sacred tongue of God! I hear thee calling and I come.
—*Confucius*

THE EVOLUTION of man and of the planet on which he dwells may be traced musically as well as spiritually. In so doing it is discovered that both tracings proceed simultaneously and along parallel paths. As a matter of fact, the two stand apart only to our limited perception. In their essence they are inseparably united, and in higher realms of being it is recognized that musical understanding and spiritual realization are identical.

"In the beginning was the Word." Both the universe and man were created by tone. The musical formula for this creative act is contained in the very first chapter of Genesis, the Book of Eternal Beginnings, and also in the first chapter of the supreme Book of the New Testament, the Gospel of St. John.

Throughout the entire universe there sounds a three-fold Song which is the Song of the Absolute. The Song is One but it possesses three aspects: Power, or harmony; the Word, or melody; and Motion, or rhythm. This universal song is literally the primordial energy by which God manifests Himself. It is truly a music, although human sensitivity is not yet such that it can be heard physically; but whether he hears it or not, man does in actual fact live, move, and have his being in a universe of tonal harmony.

[13]

The divine energies emitted by God's Song are rayed out into our universe by the twelve zodiacal Hierarchies which surround our solar system. Each of the twelve Hierarchies sounds forth a distinctive note of its own, which registers in earthly music as a note of the chromatic scale. The twelve signs belonging to the twelve Hierarchies fall into four groups according to the element to which they are related. Those belonging to the Fire and Air triplicities sing in Majors; those related to Water and Earth sing in Minors. Together they form the "Music of the Spheres." A specific creative task is performed by each of the zodiacal Hierarchies. While the tasks are different, all are manifestations of the One Universal Tone, which is the source of their energy, fount from which all music springs.

This stupendous cosmic chorus, being beyond man's perceptive capacity, is stepped down into lesser potencies by the Logos of our solar system, who is its Creator, and becomes known to this earth as Will (harmony), Wisdom (melody), and Activity (rhythm).

Hearing the music of the spheres is a transcendent initiatory experience for the spiritually illumined. As celestial tones are registered by "blessed ears that hear," so "blessed sight" registers a rainbow of colors that accompany the sounding of those tones. Plato was among the illumined ones who heard and saw these supernal glories. They are described with initiatory understanding by Shakespeare, and St. John refers to them repeatedly in recounting the revelation he received on the Isle of Patmos.

Since the tone-powered creative Fiat of the Absolute is threefold in its nature, the numbers *one, two,* and *three* are the basis of all manifestation. Confucius, the Chinese Initiate-Teacher, declared that "from One proceeds Two; from Two comes Three; and from Three come all things." Christian theology refers to this threefold power as the Holy Trinity and rightly teaches that from it all things seen and unseen come into manifestation.

One represents the point at which the true Man, Virgin Spirit, takes upon himself the first veil as he descends toward manifestation. *Two,* being dual and separative, relates to the transient or manifested state of the *One.* It is the dominant force in the present stage of human evolution. *Three* represents the Activity of the Godhead within manifested duality. It is the force that moves toward the perfection of completion under the power of *seven,* the number making up the diatonic scale.

Within physical manifestation the *Three* (triangle) rests upon the *Four* (cube), interpreted as the Three Principles manifesting in the Four Elements; or again as the threefold Spirit ruling over the fourfold personality.

Astronomically the first three signs of the Zodiac, Aries, Taurus and Gemini represent the primordial three forces which unfold progressively in the signs that follow.

When the Zodiac is taken in three groups of four each, every group starts with a Fire sign, followed by an Earth sign, then by Air and Water.

Aries	Leo	Sagittarius
Taurus	Virgo	Capricorn
Gemini	Libra	Aquarius
Cancer	Scorpio	Pisces

Reading horizontally we then find the zodiacal triplicities mentioned previously as denoting the triune cosmic force. Aries projects the seed-force into Taurus, this dual impress is then projected into Gemini; and the threefold impress repeats itself in every one of the remaining nine signs of the Zodiac.

As Aries shows the point at which the Spirit enters upon its involuntary cycle, descending into the labyrinth of manifestation, so its opposite polarity, Libra, the seventh sign of the Zodiac, is the point, or gate, through which man passes when he exchanges human concepts and the veil of flesh for cosmic knowing and the immortal raiment of the soul, whereby he can "go in and go out" at will between the spiritual realms and the physical which are their reflection. Here let us say that the Masonic fraternity admonishes its members to study music, mathematics and astronomy, these being the three fundamental sciences upon which all other studies depend.

All creations of the solar system are formed through tone emanations from the twelve Hierarchies. The alchemical basis of all things is *Fire* and *Water* in conjunction with their complementary elements of *Earth* and *Air*. These make up the zodiacal symphony to which the heavenly chorus sounds forth in the supreme chant: "And the Spirit of God (Fire) moved upon the face of the waters (Water)." This sublime chant echoes and re-echoes through the antiphonal chords of St. John's mighty song of planetary rhythm: "The Word was with God." In it the blessed Disciple transmitted for humanity something of the ecstasy voiced by the celestial Hierarchies of Aries and Taurus at creation's very beginning.

To repeat, in the combined forces of Fire, Water, Air and Earth are the Alpha and Omega of all things. This combination of powers is expressed in certain mantramic cyphers, familiar examples of which are INRI, JHVH, AMEN and the WORD. The power of the spoken word lies concealed in these cyphers, also the mystery connected with the Lost Word of Masonry. The tones carried by these letters, when properly sounded and sustained by an Initiate of the rank of St. John, become the means of effecting miraculous transmutations.

Something of their power is imparted to the Gospel of St. John, in a sublimity, a majesty unsurpassed in all the Bible. The language is sonorous, symphonic, exalted. In this connection it is interesting to note the repeated use of the numbers *three* and *seven* throughout this Gospel. By virtue of this fact, its vibrating values continue to sing their divine song down through the centuries. As the first chapter of Genesis makes plain in its recital covering the seven days of creation, our evolutionary scheme is septenary in nature. The most casual reader of the Bible does not fail to note the repetition of this number from Genesis to Revelation.

In the first of the seven creative days the fourfold power is potentially present. In the succeeding days it becomes progressively active until it reaches complete expression on the last or seventh creative day. The dominantly operative power in each of the seven days or periods is attuned to the musical keynote of one of the planets of our solar system. Thus each day adds its particular note to the grand ensemble as the innate powers of spirit become increasingly manifest. When the final or seventh note has been struck, the power of the Word that is God, the All Good, sounds forth in a glorious octave, the completed and perfect whole.

Man — A Song of God

See deep enough, and you see musically; the heart of nature being everywhere music, if you can only reach it.—Thomas Carlyle

Sometime in the future there will be a certain type of music written for the purpose of assisting mankind to resurrect memories of past lives from out the subconscious mind. This will be highly individualized music, bearing, as it were, a tonal recapitulation of past events. The basis for this assertion is the fact that human life had its beginning in music, as did the manifested universe.

As previously stated, it is through a proper blending of the Fire (masculine) and Water (feminine) principles that human life comes into manifestation. It is also through the establishment of equilibrium between these same principles that a new spiritual birth through Initiation is accomplished.

For the occult scientist birth is a threefold event. The first is physical birth, an event experienced by humanity as a whole. The second is new birth through spiritual regeneration or Initiation, an experience which has so far been attained by only the most advanced pioneers of the race. The third birth is entrance into cosmic knowing, which establishes direct contact with the activities of celestial Hierarchies. This is the stage of advancement of Masters and of Lords of Compassion, those who are assisting our planetary evolution and progression. By virtue of his having passed through this threefold birth, the great Egyptian Teacher, the God Thoth, was called by the Greeks the Thrice Great Hermes, or Hermes Trismegistus. Dante's *Divine Comedy* contains a veiled allusion to his personal experiences with stellar Hierarchies which became possible to him after he had achieved the triple birth. What one has done, another can do. The same sublime attainment awaits all who make themselves worthy.

Musical instruments embody certain tones and tonal values which pertain to celestial happenings of man's past evolution. Their origin may be traced to man's unconscious memories of truths belonging to musical evolution and the soul's sojourn in heaven between incarnations. Thus the high notes of a violin give the nearest objective approach to the tone of spirit as it is differentiated in universal consciousness. The lyre and harp are objectified concepts of certain inner powers whereby man once knew himself as a celestial instrument in tune with the Music of the Spheres. For this reason these instruments were sacred to Mystery Temples of ancient Egypt and Greece. Though now latent, the spiritual organs to which they correspond but await revivification as man reclaims his temporarily lost divine estate. The music of these instruments is such that it tends to resurrect from his subconscious mind memories of his former exalted status.

In the earliest stages of human embodiment, music was used by celestial Hierarchies to mould human bodies. In the present materialistic age music is used to awaken men's souls. Ancient music was always highly spiritual in origin and effect. With man's fall into materiality and subservience to his physical senses, it became less and less so. But the race will reawaken its neglected and sleeping spiritual powers; then music will regain the influence it once exercised over the evolving human soul. Mankind is destined to recognize and use "magic music" whereby the blind shall see, the lame shall walk, and veils of materialism will be drawn aside as communion with invisible Hosts is re-established.

Spiritual science has discovered evidence of four great periods in which human evolution has proceeded, together with the evolution of our universe and solar system. Three are in the past, and mankind now labors for liberation from materiality in the present fourth Creative Day, usually referred to as the Earth Period. Three more periods, or Days of God, are to follow, during which the personality will be transmuted into spirit and the spirit re-united with God in conscious awareness of its source and nature in Deity.

During the past three Days of God and on into the present fourth Day, cosmic Hierarchs have guided our evolution, and their work for mankind is shown in the starry heavens.

But those spiritual powers which we see today externally as stars in the heavens were in remote evolutionary epochs simply vast radiations of intelligence and power, including not merely the powers which worked upon the root of matter but also the cosmic energies which are individualized and concentrated in human emotions. The great Powers of the universe are not feelingless or emotionless beings. They differ from mankind in that their emotions are universal in scope, "weaving from star to star"; while at the same time they are intensely aware of every tiniest atom within the universe. Space and time do not hinder the workings of these mighty universal Powers. Their projected emanations created nebulae and evolved solar systems; and even when some far-off star is but a shadow of the real star which has moved onward in its orbit or perhaps disappeared from space, the spiritual emanations continue to work.

In the first great day of mankind's evolution space was dark; yet *Heat* was present in cosmic form. This period is called the Saturn Period. The Hierarchy of celestial Intelligences which had special charge of this period—for space was and is full of these Intelligences of all the Hierarchies — was a host of beings associated with what is today the constellation Leo. They are called in Christian esotericism the Lords of Flame, which is a descriptive title, "because of the brilliant luminosity of their auras and their great spiritual powers," as Max Heindel, a Rosicrucian mystic, has said: The Bible term for them is "Thrones." These beings projected into the human consciousness the seed-pattern, or archetype, of the physical body, which we possess today. This seed-pattern is rooted in a particular atom in the heart, called the "seed-atom," and man will carry this atom with him until his evolution is wholly completed. The sign Leo rules the heart, where the seed-atom is "enthroned."

The Lords of Flame sounded the tone which awoke the highest power of the Virgin Spirit (primordial mankind) into activity.

In the second cosmic Day of God the element of Air was added to the evolutionary picture and Heat became Light. In this Period the seed-pattern of the "vital body," or life-force body, was given to the Virgin Spirit. This is the "body" or principle which makes growth possible, and which also bestows freedom of movement and the power of propagation. The pattern for this body was given by the Hierarchy of Virgo. In the third Creative Day Moisture was added to Heat and Light of the two earlier Periods. The material condition resulting from this was similar to a "fire-fog," a condition belonging to nebulae in the very earliest dawn of creation.

In the third cosmic Day another Hierarchy, that of Libra, emanated from itself the seed-pattern of man's astral or emotional body.

With the dawning of the present fourth Creative Day the principle of Mind was added to the preceding three principles, namely those from which developed the physical, etheric and astral bodies. This Mind principle was activated by the Hierarchy of Sagittarius, the Lords of Mind.

In each of the four Creative Days one of the four elements came into manifestation under the power of the zodiacal triplicity to which it belongs. In the first Day, the element of Fire manifested under the combined impulses of Aries, Leo and Sagittarius, the Fire Hierarchies. The work of the first Day, therefore, produced "Fire Music." The second Day introduced the Air element through the concerted work of the Hierarchies of that element, namely Gemini, Libra and Aquarius. Theirs was "Air Music." The third Day introduced the Water element under the three Water Hierarchies: Cancer, Scorpio and Pisces. Evolution then continued under the rhythm of "Water Music." The fourth Day, our present Earth Period, received the impulses of the three Earth Hierarchies, Taurus, Virgo and Capricorn, which brought the Earth element into manifestation to the accompaniment of "Earth Music."

Truly man originates in the music of the spheres!

Due to the materialism of the present age, comparatively few realize the spiritual potential of music or the high uses to which it can be directed by those who know how to tune in to celestial harmonies. The magic attributed by legend to the music of Orpheus is destined to become an actuality for the masses.

Music is often described as the voice of spirit. This poetical expression has its foundation in reality. Virgin spirits composing the present human race were first differentiated within the heart of God through the power of the Word, which sounds the musical keynote of the universe. Each of the seven cosmic planes to which the planetary life of earth is related is sounding continuously its own keynote in harmony with the sevenfold tonal symphony of the evolutionary scheme to which we belong. Thus, as the human ego descends from the highest heaven toward physical birth it is literally bathed in music. It is projected into being by a Song of God; and the several bodies the ego builds for itself, in and through which to function, are fashioned by the music of the heavens.

For this reason it may be said that an individual's star map or horoscope showing the positions of the planetary bodies at the moment of birth is a musical score done in planetary symbols of the heavenly harmonies and dissonances as these are played into the life of the incarnating ego. A horoscope thus becomes the musical signature of a person.

Primarily, each ego is attuned to the keynote of one of the planets. Through meditation and inner work it is possible for one to discover his particular planetary keynote. As one grows spiritually this basic note increases in volume and intensity until it becomes a victorious chant that overcomes the dissonances of the squaring or opposing configurations in his stellar chart, and merges the whole into a triumphant chorale.

At all times the heavens are resonant with music sent forth by countless interweaving tones of heavenly bodies. The mystic wheel of life which shows star positions at birth records only the tones to which a particular ego responds. A "silent note" occurs in a chart when the musical emanation is too rarified for the ego's individual response.

Again, there are mighty tonal powers being rayed out through the universe from certain fixed stars, notably Sirius, Alcyone and the Pleiades, to which this earthy planet cannot as yet respond. Almost inconceivable developments await both man and the planet in the course of the atomic age that has now dawned. St. Paul made reference to these undeciphered wonders mid the stars when he declared, "There is one glory of the sun, and another glory of the moon, and another glory of the stars: for one star differeth from another star in glory" (I Cor. 15:41).

Occult science teaches that in the highest realms music is the principal motivating factor of all being. By music flowers bloom and plant life is sustained. By music celestial Beings communicate with one another; their speech is song. And by harmony all phenomena are formed and sustained. Although humanity has largely lost contact with these lofty realms, an echoing from them remains with it. In the words of Shakespeare,

> There's not the smallest orb which thou behold'st
> But in his motion like an angel sings,
> But whilst this muddy vesture of decay
> Doth grossly close it in, we cannot hear it.

MUSIC IN THE PRENATAL PERIOD

In the germ, when the first trace of life begins to stir, music is the nurse of the soul; it murmurs in the ear, and the child sleeps; the tones are companions of his dreams — they are the world in which he lives.
—*Bettina*

In the month of December there occurs in the interior heaven worlds a ceremonial termed *desire for rebirth*. (This corresponds to the time of the winter solstice.)

All egos who are to come into physical incarnation during the coming year take part in this magnificent inner-plane ritual. The esotericist knows that the human spirit or ego is never infantile. These are "adult" spirits who participate in the ceremonial of coming to birth. The divine Hierarchs lead them in a review, or recapitulation as it were, of the past epochs of their involutionary descent into matter, from the very dawn of creation, marking out for them the principal events; these are in turn correlated with the prenatal period, which is a physical recapitulation of man's past evolution. They are also shown, pictures of several possible incarnations, and they usually have a choice of two or three of these; for the ego must give its consent even to the most miserable of incarnations. It is able to do this in the high realms of the Third Heaven where it is spiritually illumined and sees the purpose of all things. Although the average ego is almost totally unconscious in the Third Heaven, and its stay is brief, it is held awake momentarily by the enfolding Intelligences of the Hierarchies while it makes its preparations for rebirth.

As the egos descend successively from the Third Heaven down through the Second and First Heavens, there is a corresponding activity in the first three prenatal months. They are bathed and sustained in the music emanating from the first, second and third groups of stellar Hierarchies. It must not be supposed that these spiritual Hierarchies are far off in the skies because the constellations are there. Space cannot delimit or define Spirit. This is why ancient seers, observing planet or star, would say, "The god (or angel) came down and spoke to me."

Modern esotericists explain this by saying that "a ray" (of the life) of the planetary Spirit descends upon the earth, appearing in human-like form to the vision of the seer, although in reality the planetary Spirit has never left its true home in the heavens. Thus also the mother and unborn child are quite literally surrounded by Angels from the Hierarchies of the skies.

These prenatal months are vitally important in the

life of an incoming ego. Therefore they must be of special significance in the lives of those who have dedicated themselves to the high privilege and serious responsibility of parenthood. The Hierarchy of Aries, whose musical keynote is B Flat Major, holds the mystery of *life itself*. The Hierarchy of Taurus, whose musical keynote is Flat Major, contains the archetypal pattern of *form*. The Hierarchy of Gemini, the Seraphim, whose musical keynote is F Sharp Major, fuses the forces of *life and form*. During these first three prenatal months the ego studies and works with these archetypal patterns that came into existence in the dawn of creation.

Throughout the first month, under Aries, the ego hovers over the mother. The music of Aries is formless. In the second month, under Taurus, the ego enters the body of the mother. The music of Taurus produces form. During the third month, under Gemini, there is an integration of spirit and form. The music of the dual sign Gemini works to conjoin the ego's spiritual and physical natures. In the fourth month, under Cancer, the ego enters into its own body. This is the time of the quickening.

Under the cosmic waters of Cancer, the Hierarchy of the Cherubim whose musical keynote is G Sharp Major, the body that is in process of formation is nourished by the waters of life. Next it is strengthened and nourished by the warming fires of love under the guidance of the Hierarchy of Leo, whose musical keynote is A Sharp Major. The forces of these two Hierarchies, Cancer and Leo, are unified and incorporated into the developing embryo under the guidance of Virgo, whose musical keynote is C Natural.

During the last three prenatal months the harmonizing forces of the Hierarchy of Libra, whose keynote is D Major, unites and polarizes the feminine forces of Scorpio, whose keynote is E Major, with the masculine forces of Sagittarius (Fire), whose musical keynote is F Major.

So is fashioned the perfect body-temple — "An house not made with hands" — which the incoming ego is to occupy during its earthly pilgrimage.

The first three months after birth the ego is surrounded and protected by the Hierarchy of Capricorn (Archangels), whose musical keynote is G Major, and Aquarius (Perfected Humanity), whose musical keynote is B Major. At this time the infant is more closely attuned to the heaven world and its celestial Beings than it is to earth and its humanity. The lights of heaven often play across a baby's face; and its Angel guardians leave their impress about it as a soft and luminous halo. During these three months immediately following birth the ego, in its infant body, is still a citizen of heaven, aware of earth only at intervals, and so it spends much time sleeping. It is conscious of inner-plane beings who come and go, mingling with the physical beings who care for its body. From three to six months of age the infant learns to associate himself clearly with the material world, and infantile clairvoyance decreases sharply at this point, although it continues to linger, to some degree, all through childhood and sometimes throughout youth.

Thus at about three months of age, the ego-in-rebirth has recapitulated the entire cycle of its past evolution, and is ready for a new cycle of experience. It has run the celestial circuit from Aries to Pisces: the Hierarchy of Aries contains the archetypal image of the god-man; the Hierarchy of Pisces manifests on earth the man "made in the image and likeness of god." Well may the Angels sing, "It is finished!"

In the work of coming to birth, the dominant note of the twelve-string cosmic symphony is sounded by the Hierarchy governing the birth month of the incoming ego.

Observe, however, that during the prenatal period, and up to and including the three postnatal months, the twelve creative Hierarchies were divided into four groups of three each, which we may term "trinities" rather than "triplicities." The first trinity consisted of Aries, Taurus and Gemini, with the major influence operating through the third of these signs, Gemini; the corresponding element being Air. The second trinity consisted of Cancer, Leo and Virgo, with Virgo the dominant influence, and Earth the element. The third trinity consisted of Libra, Scorpio and Sagittarius, their forces flowing through the element of Fire. The fourth trinity, consisting of Capricorn, Aquarius and Pisces, worked chiefly through the element of Water.

Thus we have the four elements of Air, Earth, Fire and Water as the basis of creation. Herein is found the significance of the WORD of John's Gospel: "The Word was in the beginning, and that very Word was with God, and God was the Word. The same was in the beginning with God" (John I: 1, 2 Lasma version). This Word is the Elohim of the Book of Genesis. How high and holy is the prenatal period! And how sublime and far-reaching the work of fashioning man's body temple!

PRIMARY COLORS IN RELATION TO PRENATAL DEVELOPMENT

A continuous evolution during the prenatal period synchronizes form, color and tone — a chromatic scale of color as well as of tone. The first three months the ego responds dominantly to blue tones; the next three months, to tones of yellow; the seventh, eighth and ninth months, to red. After birth, a shade resulting from the blending of these three primary colors reveals in an aura of gleaming color the ego's evolutionary status.

In relation to the Trinity, blue is the Father color; yellow, that of the Christ; red, that of the Holy Spirit. We discover, therefore, that in prenatal development the power of the Father is required to inaugurate the formation of a new body; the cohesive principle of love, to carry it forward through its second stage; the activating principle of the Holy Spirit, to complete the third and last stage immediately preceding entry upon an independent physical existence.

It is only when we consider more than one series of attributes and qualities assigned to the Trinity, and observe how they harmonize and support one another in relation to the logical processes in nature as we can observe them at certain points, that we arrive at a conviction that the assignments of colors or tones or principles to Beings or to aspects of Beings, or to phases of development, are neither arbitrary nor pure abstractions invented by human intellect. They are realities existing in the very essence of things.

MUSICAL HOROSCOPES

One of the most euphonious of all phrases is the *Music of the Spheres*. At a certain stage of his progressive attainment, every Initiate undergoes an "illumination by sound" in which the Music of the Spheres becomes for him a living reality. As Dr. Rudolf Steiner has said:

If we succeed in pushing away the inner barrier between the etheric body and the physical body, and if we are then able to look down into the etheric body and into the physical body, we hear a music resounding in the etheric body and also in the physical body. These sounds are the echo of the harmony of the spheres which man took into himself when he came down from the divine-spiritual world into the physical world.

One of the coming developments of that long-lost science of musical therapy — a science now rapidly being recovered — will be musical horoscopes. These will be based on the correlations between the twelve-tone chromatic scale and the twelve zodiacal Hierarchies that surround our solar system; and also between the seven-tone diatonic scale and the seven planets (including this earth) which belong to our particular system. The Bible refers to these planets as the seven Spirits before the throne of God. Each note of the chromatic scale sounds forth the keynote of one of the twelve zodiacal signs while the notes of the diatonic scale key in with the tones of the planets. As this fascinating aspect of astrological music is developed, we shall realize increasingly how literally true is the poetic reference to a body suffering physical or mental ills as "sweet bells jangled, out of tune and harsh."

By setting one's radical chart to music, his birth song may be heard. The trines and squares of the planetary aspects will sound forth as harmony and discord respectively. The so-called evil aspects are the discords we have created in the past by striking wrong keys or from not having learned which are the right ones. The concords, on the other hand, are joyful proclamations of successful harmonization with the universal rhythms through trials overcome and lessons learned.

It was through the scientific application of such basic facts that Pythagoras, perhaps the most proficient as well as the most-celebrated musical therapist of all time, effected such marvelous cures of bodies, minds and souls. With music's magic he treated every type of illness. Destructive emotions of fear, anger, sensuality and so forth were "played down" whereas ennobling impulses of the soul were "played up" to a degree where they became healing and regenerative.

Aristotle conceived of music as including astronomy, and so taught it. Plato defined music as "moral law." "Music," said he, "gives a soul to the universe, wings to the mind, flight to the imagination, a charm to sadness, gaiety and life to everything. It is the essence of order and leads to all that is just and good and beautiful."

Such is the divine mission of music. When employed in conjunction with the science of the stars, and applied to an individual in accordance with his life's pattern as revealed by his birth chart, a phase of healing will be practiced that will be worthy of the wisdom taught in the ancient Temples of Light. Musical horoscopes will be a part of that practice, for in both his inner and outer constitution man is fashioned in accordance with the musical motion of the stars. Man is, in very truth, a "song of God."

> Great Nature had a million words
> In tongues of trees and songs of birds,
> But none to breathe the heart of man,
> 'Till music filled the pipes o' Pan.
>
> —*Henry Van Dyke*

Chapter II

PRE-HISTORIC ORIGINS

MUSIC OF LEMURIA

Music . . . a kind of inarticulate, unfathomable speech, which leads us to the edge of the infinite.—Thomas Carlyle

THE ELEMENTS of Fire, Air, Water and Earth are most important in earth's evolutionary scheme; in fact, without these four elements life upon this planet would be impossible. Fire was first discovered and used by man in the days of Lemuria. It was, therefore, the dominant element connected with the Lemurian race and a main factor in their initiatory ceremonials. Ability to walk on red-hot coals and to hold balls of fire in one's hands is a fragmentary memory from ancient days still retained by some primitive peoples.

The music which accompanied Lemurian Fire Ceremonials was both weird and wild, for it was attuned to the rhythm of up-leaping flames. In this music jazz, so popular in the world today, had its origin. The Lemurian's desire body needed a quickening so the Great Ones used this peculiar rhythmic music to stimulate its activity. In the course of time this awakened inner fire force led to misdirected practices that reacted on the corresponding planetary fire-forces, resulting in the destruction of the Lemurian continent by volcanic action.

Human beings who inhabited ancient Lemuria had very little resemblance to those of our time. During the early part of that epoch, remote by many millions of years, their bodily form was merely embryonic. Over a long evolutionary span it went through successive transformations until, in late Lemuria, it had assumed a shape somewhat similar to its present contour, although its texture was very different. Before it condensed into physical sub-

[29]

stance the vehicles of this early humanity were rather tenuous and plastic. It might, in fact, be regarded as almost a shadow form.

Hence, the body had not yet developed to the point where the ego could become in-dwelling. It was only magnetically linked to its body and was, therefore, in a free state that enabled it to come and go at will. Mind as we know it today had not yet come into existence for it. Infant humanity — and it was really infantile — was under the direction of superior Hierarchies, spiritual Beings whom we are wont to call *gods*.

Nevertheless, primitive Lemurians lived in close harmony with nature. Their life was intimately interwoven with, and actually an integral part of the nature forces themselves. Their inner sight was open to the myriad activities of invisible (to us) creatures that make up the life side of nature in its totality, while their inner hearing registered the sublime harmonies to which nature moves, and in and through which it carries on its manifold operations. Also, it was in accordance with the underlying laws of nature that their original bodies were fashioned, developed and sustained.

When mankind is sufficiently spiritualized to recognize the relation of music to his evolution, he will discover how celestial harmonies emanating from the zodiacal Hierarchies, our starry guardians, exercised a formative influence on his every stage of development; and that every step has been accompanied by celestial orchestration suited to each creative process.

Man in the making was bi-sexual. The masculine and feminine polarities, now focused cosmically in the Sun and Moon respectively, exercised an equal influence over the plastic bodies of early humanity. But this was at a time when the earth and the Moon were still parts of the solar orb. At a later stage when the earth was thrown off from the Sun and, at a still later date, when the Moon was thrown off from the earth, these two polarities ceased to have an equal and balanced expression in individual human beings. Some responded preponderantly to the positive pole centered in the Sun, while others responded to the negative pole focused in the Moon. Eventually, this resulted in the division of humanity into two separate sexes with man and woman appearing upon the scene.

Then it was that harmonies emanating from stellar Hierarchies became differentiated into two rhythms now known as *major* and *minor*. Major tones, masculine in potency and objective in character, were projected to humanity by means of the Sun force. Minor notes, feminine in quality and subjective in nature, were directed through the force of the Moon. Whereas man had hitherto evolved under the divided rhythms of a single scale, he now became subject to two. The one keyed to major tones tended to draw him into conditions of increasing density; the one keyed to minors drew his soul into more intimate contact with powers of the spirit.

As the Lemurian Epoch was predominantly under the influence of the Moon, its music was keyed to the subtler nuances of the minor. It was strange, plaintive, unearthly music. Echoes of it persist in the music of Java and other South Sea Islands, these lands being remnants of the Lemurian continent.

The inmost nature of any people may be divined by entering understandingly into their music. By no other means can the quality of their life and the stage of their development be so accurately determined. Unless we are able to visualize the plastic, fluidic bodies of those early Lemurians we shall never understand the influence exerted upon them by music. It literally gave outline and features to their developing vehicles. Nature's enveloping forces flowed through them unimpeded. They dwelt amid the giant trees of their land, and its mighty groves were sacred areas wherein seasonal festivals were observed. Initiatory rites of their sacred seasons were glorious events set to music, that is, to the harmony of the spheres.

Lemurian Temple dancers duplicated the movements and rhythms of heavenly orbs, their "music of motion" being audible to the dancing devotees. Certain spiritual centers or "lights" within their bodies were awakened by means of these dances performed in the highest reverence and deepest devotion. The performers were always chosen from among the most highly evolved of Temple aspirants. Forest Temples were to Lemurians their Holy of Holies. In these sacred shrines occurred the principal events of their lives. These embraced birth, Initiation or spiritual illumination, and death — events corresponding to the three steps of unfoldment in all esoteric schools and to the first three degrees of fraternal lodges. It was in forest Temples and under angelic guidance that propagation of the race took place at times in accord with proper stellar rhythms, the music of which was audibly absorbed and transmitted to the function of body building.

Sensitive Lemurian egos were especially responsive to the power of love. Consciousness was unbroken as the egos had not yet descended deeply enough into material existence to draw a veil between outer and inner planes of being. Hence, death as we know it was unknown. When bodies had served their term of usefulness they were laid aside in much the same way as some animals periodically shed their skins. A body generated under such conditions was perfectly attuned to the ego's own particular star note. By the power of that note it was able to renew or discard its body at will. Disease had not yet become an affliction, so life was a joyous song and earth was still a reflection of the Edenic Garden.

Since the Lemurian race was ruled by the Moon, it responded strongly to that orb's ever-changing phases. At the time of New Moons and Full Moons powerful forces were released; so then it was that they observed their mystic initiatory rites. These were not directed to inner planes as now but to the outer, since Lemurian advancement depended primarily upon developing objective functioning. Music was a potent factor in enabling them to make a necessary descent into matter. With this descent differentiation between the sexes became more marked, and was accomplished through the Major and Minor rhythms that accompany the Full Moon and New Moon respectively. On nights of the New Moon the feminine forces were precipitated through celestial minors; on nights of the Full Moon the masculine forces were precipitated by means of majors.

Later, when Lemurian humanity had entered fully upon physical existence and when, through the fall into the separative sense life of the material world, birth and death marked the differentiated phases of existence, entrance into physical manifestation was accompanied by music set to major harmonies; while entrance into inner worlds, through the gate we call death, was keyed to minor chords.

Thus we see how profoundly true it is that man is a musical being. His origin is in the spoken Word. By sound was he sustained and by music was he evolved. What he registered subconsciously in Lemuria he will one day consciously know. Then he will no longer consider music as an art more or less detached from life, nor will he think of it primarily as a subject for esthetic delight only. Instead, he will recognize music as a vital factor in the physical, mental, emotional and spiritual evolution of the whole human race.

MUSIC OF ATLANTIS

Music is the art of the prophets, the only art that can calm the agitations of the soul; it is one of the most magnificent and delightful presents God has given us.—*Luther*

Water was the principal element associated with Atlantis, where man was being taught to control his emotions and to develop his physical faculties. In that continent psychism attained to a stage greater than ever known before or since, and Atlantean music was a factor in the development of psychic faculties. Much of this music was solemn and serious, sometimes reaching heights of imposing grandeur. Its undulating waves of melody were comparable to rhythmic music now heard in the ingoing and outflowing tides of the sea. The Sun never shone clearly in Atlantis. The atmosphere was always heavy with mist. In this mist-laden atmosphere vaporous figures from other planes were easily discernible, a condition which aided tremendously in awakening and developing psychic faculties. The Atlantean Period came to a close when the continent was destroyed by water.

[33]

The transition from Lemuria to Atlantis was marked by increasing density of the atmosphere, more solidified physical bodies, and human consciousness focused more definitely in the material world. Humanity was now losing that beautiful and almost continuous communion with angelic Hosts which had been enjoyed by the Lemurians. Consequently, there was a corresponding loss in perception of celestial harmonies. However, at this stage of its development it had not lost contact with inner worlds to such a degree as to deny or even doubt the existence of the Music of the Spheres, whether it was actually heard or not. Such denial did not come until the deep materialism of our present era. Hence, Atlantean Temple Initiates, priests and priestesses of eternal wisdom, performed their sacred rites in full accord with celestial rhythms.

Atlantean Temples were really universities where man's physical, mental and spiritual faculties were nurtured and developed. To the degree that he ceased to live in rapport with supernal worlds did his body become subject to inharmony and disease, so it was largely an Initiate-Teacher who tuned in with an individual's star note in order to replace the latter's inharmony with harmony. To this end music, the great healing panacea, was administered in these Temples.

Atlantean peoples were much more susceptible to the remedial effects of rhythm than is humanity of the present day. They could draw upon the pulsing life forces of growing plants and appropriate them for the revitalization and renewal of their bodies. They could also transfer these energies from one plant to another, thus augmenting the strength of the weak or afflicted by that of the strong and healthy. The throbbing currents of life emitted specific tones as they surged upward. The Atlanteans could hear these sounds and transcribe them into music so perfectly attuned to the rhythms of the plants that it possessed dynamic healing efficacy. In time, therefore, musical therapy became one of the principal branches of Temple instruction.

Speech was developed by the Atlanteans, a sort of

singing speech. Their intoned words projected power into any object named, and by that power the object could be reshaped in accordance with an individual's will. The chants and mantrams of all ancient religions had their origin in this *singing speech.* Temple priests and their advanced disciples could also hear the musical keynotes of natural objects and were able, by means of the power this gave them, to perform miracles of transformation. Herein originated numerous myths and legends regarding the earliest civilizations of our present Fifth Root Race, the Aryan peoples. In the Golden Age of Atlantis leadership was conferred upon the most spiritually developed Temple neophytes, who were accorded honor and reverence by the laity. Kingship was a Temple Degree to which only the worthiest might aspire, for the Initiate-King was second only to the High Priest.

It will be seen that in the Atlanteans' practically unlimited power lay the seed of ultimate decadence and destruction. The temptation to misuse that power was for them well nigh irresistible. With the unfoldment of their desire natures and a concomitant growth in selfish interests, abilities which originally functioned under the direction of the Hierarchies of Light were transferred to those of the Shadow. Conditions heralding chaos and disintegration — similar to those manifesting in the world today — became prevalent. Such conditions are ever indicative of the "beginning of the end.' The *singing speech* of consecrated Temple-Initiates was made over to evil and destructive ends. Literally, "blasts of tone," attuned to the keynote of a person or an object, were used to ruthlessly destroy human life and property.

Man's knowledge of celestial harmonies in currents of majors and minors has been noted previously. With the increasing depravity of the Atlanteans, consonances and dissonances became more and more sharply differentiated. A strange and sinister music was the result, a music capable of producing disease, loss of memory and even insanity. "Dark Circles" composed of Temple-neopyhtes working under Shadow influences were able to utter blasts of tone that could drive an ego out of its body, frequently causing the person's permanent obsession or death. These facts are mentioned merely to bring out the far-reaching powers of sound.

Only a remnant of the Atlanteans were saved. In biblical terminology, Noah and his family survived the Flood. This remnant became the seed of the present Aryan race. Upon the new continent to which the remnant migrated the Sun shone clearly, and for the first time man came to enjoy an oxygenated atmosphere such as we have today. Humanity of this race received the supreme gift of mind, the link which will enable him to become as the gods. The great work of the Aryans is to spiritualize and develop Christed minds. As mind is correlated with the element of Air, it is by means of air that its greatest progress will be made. Should there be another destruction of this planet after its lessons have been learned, it will come about through that element.

The human race is destined to recover the celestial harmonies it lost on Atlantis. This it will do through its Christed mind, and music is the foremost factor in that attainment. Throughout the centuries the Great Ones have sent to earth some of their more advanced musical Initiates to aid man in spiritualizing his mind. Such was the purpose of Haydn's *Creation,* of Handel's *Messiah* and of Bach's magnificent *Passions.* This development is under the Lords of Mind who belong to the Hierarchy of Sagittarius, the sign which holds the pattern of higher mind and its spiritual mysteries. The Hierarchy's service to man is to quicken his spiritual incentives and encourage his aspirations until he gains ascendency over his lower carnal mind.

The keynote of Sagittarius is F Major and the keynote of the earth is also F Major. Many of nature's sounds, therefore, are set to this key. This is the reason why compositions in F Major are especially relaxing to tired nerves; also effective in restoring a fatigued body and in calming a distracted mind.

By rhythms of F Major the Lords of Mind bestowed germinal mind upon nascent humanity; and by its further use they are bringing that mind to the point where it can transmit to men's outer personality the spirit-image within themselves. Such will become pioneers of the coming Sixth Root Race, and among them will arise a type of music possessing qualities that heal and illumine. All forward-looking movements are preparatory schools for the New Age. To the extent that the minds of neophytes become spiritualized will they receive, through tone and rhythm, those higher powers which are waiting to be bestowed upon man.

Chapter III

ANCIENT ORIGINS

MUSIC OF SUMERIA

If you learn music, you'll learn history. If you learn music, you'll learn mathematics. If you learn music, you'll learn most all there is to learn.

—Edgar Cayce

SUMERIAN CIVILIZATION has been traced back to 8000 B.C. It is recorded that "Euridu, Lagash, Ur, Uruh, Larsa have already an immemorial past when they first appear in history." An inscription discovered in the ancient city of Nippur, a principal seat of this earliest known of all empires, describes Sumerian as reaching from the Persian Gulf to the Mediterranean or Red Sea. This half-fabled land attained to a civilization and culture which, before its conquest by Semetic peoples, produced a veritable Golden Age.

It was in this fabled land, which lay between the Euphrates and the Tigris rivers, that in the fourth millenium B.C. the early Sumerian kings established a civilization of unparalleled splendor. Later, a portion of this land was named Mesopotamia by the Romans. Here Nebuchadnezzar of Bible fame knew the glory that was Babylon, with its hanging gardens which were numbered among the Seven Wonders of the ancient world. In fact, the beauty and luxuriant fertility of this area has caused it to be known through the ages as the Garden of Eden of this earth planet. The remnants of that ancient splendor are known today as the kingdom of Iraq.

In the third century B.C. a Babylonian priest, Berosus, described this enchanting land, stating among other things that in it religion and magic were one. He told of weird creatures, half fish and half men, who came up out of the Red Sea; and who, under the guidance of Ea, the water god and patron of learning, established the first metropolis, the city of Eridu. An old Sumerian poem describes these creatures as coming from "the land of Shinar" (place of light) and as "wearing no garments and eating herbs."

For an occultist the enigma of the Sumerians is solved by the knowledge that their high culture had its origin in Atlantis. They were part of the great Fourth Root Race which had been led from the doomed continent in order to escape destruction, for they qualified as pioneers of the succeeding Aryan civilization. As a group they possessed unusual extension of normal faculties, a development they later lost and which is now practically forgotten by all but a few individuals here and there.

Archeologists and scientists come near the truth when they state that "ancient Sumerians may have been linking language between the early Basque-Caucasian and early Mongolian groups." And again, in their surmise that "eight or ten thousand years ago there extended over Southern Europe, language groups which have completely vanished before the Aryan (Fifth Root Race) tongues."

The fanciful legend of Sumerian origins as related by Berosus conceals inner truths of profound significance. "Half fish and half men" refers to the Hierarchy of Pisces that worked intimately with the early Sumerians. Pisces is a feminine water sign. The patron of learning was Ea, the Water Spirit. Pisces carries the influence of Venus, Jupiter and Neptune, high spiritual and artistic forces that played upon the Sumerian Golden Age. The Fish-God Dagan of later biblical times was a throwback to this Piscean influence. An understanding and demonstration of the occult significance of music was part of the educational system of that Golden Age. To rightly comprehend what this statement implies, it is necessary to know something about the Race Spirits of nations and what their work involves.

Race Spirits are exalted Beings who assume the responsibility of serving as celestial guardians of various nations. Above each national group is its archetypal pattern, a divine image which outlines the past, present and future development of the people. The Race Spirit assists in lifting and leavening the mass consciousness of a nation that it may be capable of its highest attainment. Ofttimes this must come, as in the lives of individuals, through sorrow and pain. Possessing cosmic wisdom, the Race Spirit sees beyond existing limitations and envisions the people's ultimate and permanent good.

Every nation is keyed to one of the twelve zodiacal Hierarchies. The Race Spirit is a channel for the reception and transmission of the heavenly forces and harmonies they send forth. For this reason a Race Spirit is said to express itself in the language and music of a people. Their folk music is of particular significance because it is the "musical heartbeat" of the inhabitants and is in complete attunement with the zodiacal Hierarchy.

A person is bound to his native land by the potencies of music and language. The national anthem of every nation is in harmony with its initial rhythm. Seldom can even an insensitive person listen unmoved to the strains of his country's national air, for it plays upon his very heartstrings. Before the separative tendency of nations can be broken down there must be a universal language and a new music, a music not centered primarily in the exaltation of national virtues but in the Fatherhood of God and the Brotherhood of Man.

Properly developing the seven ductless glands to spiritual functioning will have much to do with preparing man to become a citizen of this "larger and freer earth." Development of the power center in the larynx bound him to his Race Spirit. Development of the thyroid gland will help to free him — for the thyroid is attuned to Mercury, bearer of wisdom and messenger of the gods.

A Sumerian hymn containing the oldest form of musical notation yet known, has been discovered in Asshur. Based upon the theme of the creation of man, the words and music are of majestic stateliness and beauty. The symbols of this notation are composed of cuneiform characters, declared by many students of the subject to be undecipherable. But one authority, Dr. Curt Sachs, comes near to occult truth in his assertion that the symbols do not represent single notes but a short melodic pattern. When science eventually accepts the reality of the Music of the

Spheres, in such ancient treasures will be found new meanings as yet unperceived. Man was made in the image and likeness of God through the instrumentality of the twelve zodiacal Hierarchies. These melodic Patterns sound the keynote of those Hierarchies. The music of the *Creation Hymn* possesses an intricate scale formation and there is a cryptic line inscribed at its beginning: "The secret let the learned reveal to the learned." Dr. Sachs further notes that Sumerian music was not bound to a five-tone scale but had both chromatic and enharmonic alternatives.

It appears that the three principal instruments used by Sumerians for Temple work were the drum, the flute and the harp. The *balag* or god-drum was used prominently in the Temple dedicated to Enki at Eridu to "assuage tears and soften sighing"; and in processionals to "calm and uplift the people of the city." On holy occasions the priestess with the drum summoned the gods, so the drummer was recognized as an important personage, one who understood the power and effect of vibratory rhythms upon man's chain of vehicles. Mention has been made previously of the correlation between percussion instruments and the desire body. The fasting chant of the Temple of Enki reads: "To the house of God with lament and prayer let us go with the hallowed drum." The drum and its office belonged to the outer fore-court of the Temple, the place of worship for the masses. The flute was used in the inner court; the harp, within the sacred place.

About 3000 B.C. the Sumerians were guided by the Holy Priest-King Gudea, who abode in the city of Lagash. The chief musicians of the Temple were directly under his instruction. These were singers and chanters and were both masculine and feminine, *nar* and *naru*. Statues of Gudea bear the record that so happy was the lot of the people no corpse was buried without music. The following lines from a poem by Gudea entitled *Music's Ministry* are quoted by Francis Galpin in one of his works on Sumerian music:

> To fill with joye the Temple Court
> And chase the cities's gloome awaie,
> The harte to still the passion's calme,
> Of weeping eyes the teares to staie.

A seven-note flute, *imine*, was played for hymns of adoration and penitence, and the processional intoned the chant: "Bring only into the fore-courts the drum and the seven-note." This flute was used to make contact with the seven planets of our solar system.

Temple harps varied from eleven to fifteen strings, though simpler and smaller instruments of four or five strings were used by the general public. *Eleven* appears to have been the most important number to Sumerians. It was found on a lyre, *al-gar*, in the Temple of Enki, where it was said "the holy al-gar sings in reverence." In a hymn to Ishtar of 2100 B.C. are the words "I will speak to Thee with the *al-gar* whose voice is sweet." These sacred harps were exquisite instruments made of gold and lapis lazuli set with precious stones. Enki, the God of Music, sang its praises and taught its use. Of it was said, "It glittered like the stars by day, it was holy by night, it poured forth song."

The spiritual life of the Sumerians was centered in the Temple, the "House of Life." Every Temple had its lofty tower or ziggurat. In its highest dome was a small chapel furnished with a golden bed and table. This was the meeting place between heaven and earth, a sacred spot where the chosen priestess received revelations of the gods to the strains of her harp. Abuse of this holy rite, together with general decadence that came later, is biblically described in the destruction of the Tower of Babel.

The royal standard of Ur, the city of Abraham, depicts a royal banquet in which the Priest-King Gudea and his skilled musicians are driving gloom away from the city. Esotericists understand that it was by the magic of music that a cloud of evil and error which enveloped the city was being transmuted, and the city's vibratory rhythms correspondingly raised. This important function of music will someday be rediscovered and used.

In the art of Sumeria is a representation of herdsmen leading submissive wild animals of the desert and domesticated creatures of the countryside to the accompaniment of the musical magic of lute and lyre — another application of music due for restoration in the New Age. A Babylonian stone of 1600 B.C., now in the Louvre, portrays seven men accompanied by seven different animals bringing offerings to Lagash and the Holy Gudea.

The Golden Age of Sumerian art was approximately 3000 to 1500 B.C., a renaissance which occurred about 500 B.C. in Assyria and Babylonia. However, the magnificence and splendor of these two empires was largely material. The spiritual powers of the Initiate-Ruler Gudea and the musical magic of his day were all but forgotten. They had already become no more than beautiful fables, and remain so to this day.

In the days of Ashurbahipal (658 B.C.) another type of harp, the *zakkal,* was in use. Its strains, however, were not for the purpose of communion with celestial realms but to celebrate the triumphs, conquests and aggressions of warriors. The mystic tones of the instrument had been silenced. A civilization founded upon materialism cannot endure. By its very nature it is impermanent and so passes away. Consequently, in 606 B.C. Ninevah, the great Assyrian city, fell before the triumphant march of the Aryans.

One by one the golden lands of Atlantis lost their evolutionary opportunity. The Fourth Root Race had been weighed in the cosmic balance and been found wanting. Another race followed, the Aryan Fifth Root Race which has reached a point where it is now being tried in the balance as were the Atlanteans before their disappearance. Out of the old and into the new race came a very high Initiate-Teacher to set the latter on the High Road. That Teacher was Abraham of the famed city of Ur of the Chaldees. "Now the Lord had said unto Abram, Get thee out of thy country, and from thy kindred, and from thy father's house, unto a land that I will shew thee."

The Music of China

When I was born the others laughed, I cried;
But others wept — I did the laughing when I died.
Birth is a joyful thing except to him who greets the dawn.
Ah, we would weep at birth and smile at death, I know,
If love of life did not deceive us so.
—*Translated from the Chinese*

If one should desire to know whether a kingdom is well governed, if its morals are good or bad, the quality of its music will furnish the answer.
—*Confucius*

Most like the music of Atlantis is the music of China, where the former's civilization is perpetuated through direct descent. China was the home of various Atlantean races whose culture was flourishing there when the last remnants of the mother continent were submerged something over ten thousand years ago. So the Chinese are correct in claiming that their music is the oldest in the world.

The close connection between the racial development of a people, their music, and the instruments devised for its expression, is clearly and strikingly evident in China. The philosophical concept held by the Chinese is that the harmonious action of the heavens playing upon the earth calls forth a corresponding musical expression. Thus, the movement of the starry vault and of the changing seasons is recognized as composing a sublime cosmic symphony. On the basis of this lovely and noble concept they have builded their philosophy of life. Consequently, the earliest religion of this mystic land was actually founded upon the movement of the stars, the science of numbers and the magic of music.

It was due to its tremendous power that for ages the Chinese kept their music under state supervision to guard against any stealthy introduction of tones contrary to their rigid ordinance. Though adversely criticized by Western writers, this restriction will be found to be of great value when comprehended esoterically. It can be seen that so great a power is safe only with the pure in heart and the spiritually illumined.

During China's Golden Age music was a sacred art. Even emperors were proud to be associated with it. Fo-Hi,

[44]

one of their earliest sages, is said to have invented the *kin,* a stringed instrument still in use. As late as A.D. 364 Ngai-Ti banned all weak or unworthy music. Theirs is an intricate system of eighty-four scales, each having a special philosophical significance.

Sacred hymns and folklore comprise the music of the people, and they have been transmitted without alteration from time immemorial. To a mythical bird, *fung-hoang,* and its mate is ascribed the invention of tones and half-tones: the whole tones by the male, the half-tones by the female. The former imply, so the Chinese affirm, perfect things like heaven, sun, man; to the latter, imperfect things like earth, moon, woman.

The Chinese taste for bizarre rhythm, so incomprehensible to western ears, is part of their heritage from Atlantis, where the evolutionary requirements were so different from those of modern Occidentals.

Ancient tradition always depicts a true Chinese musician as blind. Esoterically, this implies that his gift of the divine art is so completely guided by, and dedicated to, hosts of celestial guardians that both his sight and consciousness are focused above and beyond the objective world. This is understandable when we realize that ancient China was steeped in the lore of the Ancient Wisdom. The people were taught by Atlantean sages that the heavens are reflected in the earth; and that the more deeply man penetrates the heart of science and the arts, the closer is he attuned to celestial verities.

Chinese music, being based upon the Music of the Spheres, was made the subject of numerous allegorical comparisons. *Twelve, seven* and *five* are the principal numerical rhythms of the heavens in relation to the earth, so these numbers were the rhythms upon which the music was based. Various writings refer to the twelve signs, the twelve tones, twelve moons, twelve emperors and twelve strings. About forty-six hundred years ago the "Yellow Emperor" invented the scale of twelve semitones. In concord with the five best-known planets, the Chinese evolved the five-degree scale, the pentatonic) of G A C D E. Each note bore a name as follows: Emperor, Prime Minister,

Subject People, State Affairs and Picture of the Universe. Knowing the occult potency of music, they used these notes to further the welfare of the office or the person to which they were related. The last one, Picture of the Universe, had reference to the powers of extended vision through Initiation. Their Wise Ones recognized that if the mysteries of rhythm were to come into the possession of irresponsible or morally undeveloped individuals, it would result in "a crash of matter and a wreck of worlds." And so, as the Chinese nation descended deeper and deeper into materiality, these mysteries were gradually withdrawn from the ken of the people as a whole.

It was a Confucian doctrine that good government was not possible without music. An instance of how the Chinese drew upon its magic powers in the conduct of affairs of state, and even in connection with their military operations, is recorded in one of their ancient history books. It tells how one Liu Kun was defending Chin Yang against the Tartars. When the city reached its lowest point of resistance, Liu mounted a tower at midnight and played wandering airs on a Tartar pipe. Thereupon the barbarians stood at the doors of their tents, their hearts filled with homesickness. In the morning all the great hordes of them were gone.

The origin and symbolic use of early Chinese musical instruments are fascinating in the extreme. Legendary history traces them back as far as 43,000 B.C. China claims that musical instruments are one of the six major contributions she has made to the world, classing them with such prehistoric gifts as the institution of marriage, language, the science of divination, writing and the domestication of animals.

Perhaps the *sheng,* named for the phoenix bird that renews its life from its own ashes, is the oldest. This instrument, a favorite of Confucius, is held sacred, being used almost entirely for holy seasonal convocations and in funeral processions. It is a wind instrument which originally had twenty-four pipes, thus being attuned to the positive-negative, masculine-feminine aspects of the twelve zodiacal signs. Again, the Chinese refer to the eight points of the compass and the eight seasons of the year, for in accordance with their mysticism there are eight substances upon earth which reflect or give forth the eight keys that express all the changes and permutations occurring in the universe. These substances are stone, metal, silk, bamboo, wood, skin, gourds and clay. Stone reflects the keynote of the winter (solstice); metal, of the autumn (equinox); silk, the summer (solstice).

The *sheng* was invented by a woman ruler of China who, tradition records, lived and reigned during the days of Noah and the Flood. This bears out the Ancient Wisdom teaching that China was part of the Atlantean continent that was not destroyed by that Flood. The influence of the *sheng* was to "check evil passions, rectify the heart and guide the action of the body." In the light of such moral reaction, Confucius declared that "a wise man seeks by music to strengthen the weakness of his soul; the thoughtless one uses it to stifle his fears." There is no doubt but what the philosophical-musical conceptions of Pythagoras were intimately connected with the sacred teachings of ancient China.

There is a hymn dedicated to the "Most Holy Ancient Sage Confucius" that is (or was) used in Confucian celebrations. In it is to be found what is, perhaps, the oldest written music in the world. The celebrations are (or were) observed at the time of the Spring and Autumn Equinoxes, and were believed to receive their mystic power from being attuned to the keynotes of these Sacred Seasons. Spiritual scientists are aware of the fact that at the four turning points of the year the earth is charged with a spiritual inflow which lifts its rhythmic cadence and thus changes its vibratory keynote. This teaching was long ago given to an aspirant when he had become sufficiently sensitized to tune in to the Music of the Spheres. The hymn to Confucius had six divisions to accompany a like number of ceremonial steps. They were:

1. Receiving the approaching spirit. 2. First presentation of offerings. 3. Second offering. 4. Third offering. 5. Removal of offerings. 6. Escorting the spirit back.

When rightly performed, music in certain keys is a

strong factor in the materialization of disembodied spirits. As the New Age approaches, it is on "wings of song" that we shall be reunited with our loved ones who have passed beyond the veil. Then we will join with them in a triumphant chorus proclaiming that there is no death. In 2277 B.C. it was stated that in the College of Mandarins at Peking there were twenty-two authors on the dance and music; twenty-three on ancient music; twenty-four on solemn occasions. The mandarins of music were considered superior to those of mathematics, thus indicating how highly the powers of music were rated. Van Aalst, an authority on Chinese music, gives the following beautiful interpretation of China's conception of music:

According to Chinese ideas, music rests on two fundamentals, spiritual principle and substantial form. Unity is above, it is heaven. Plurality is below, it is earth. The spiritual principle (in music) is above, the material principle is below. Therefore when the material principle of music—that is—, the instrument—is clearly and rightly illustrated, the corresponding spiritual principle that is the essence, the sounds of music (keynotes) becomes perfectly manifest and the State's affairs are successfully conducted.

MUSIC OF INDIA

Music in the best sense does not require novelty; nay, the older it is, and the more we are accustomed to it, the greater its effect.—*Goethe*

Music moves us, and we know not why; we feel the tears, but cannot trace the source. Is it the language of some other state, born of its memory? For what can wake the soul's strong instinct of another world like music?
—*L. E. Landon*

For an Occidental to understand Hindu music it is necessary for him to realize that it springs out of a consciousness that is much closer to the subjective side of life than his own. The most outstanding characteristics of the people of India is an awareness of spiritual reality. It is, therefore, inevitable that her approach to music, to a concept of its nature and function, is spiritual rather than merely aesthetic. "According to Indian pandits," writes Ethel Rosenthal in her book entitled History of Indian Music, "musicians must possess firm devotion to God and must be pure in mind and body, for unless they realize the spiritual power of music, they will be unable to gauge the science underlying their art."

[48]

Perhaps the nation's most famous composer and singer was Tyagaraja, who has been called the Beethoven of Indian music. This noted musical sage was an idealist who lived a saintly life. His worship of the God Rama and his dedication to the patron saint of music, Narada, were equal in intensity and devotion. According to native music critics, the hymns of this holy man rank with the Psalms of David and with Thomas A'Kempis' *Imitation of Christ*. It is stated that they are "the last word on the theory and practice of devotion, music and self-culture . . . They reveal the wonderful evolution of the soul of a neophyte right onwards until he reaches the goal . . . He was an undaunted social reformer of the true type, a fearless speaker of the truth and a peerless teacher. His hymns are so sublime, so soul-reaching, that his followers reverently speak of them as 'Tyagapanishads,' for to them they are as sacred as Holy Writ."

Another of ancient India's holy musicians was Jayadera, author of the *Gita Govinda* or *Divine Herdsman*. This work, called a Sanskrit *Song of Solomon*, was translated into English by Sir Edwin Arnold as the *Indian Song of Songs*. It recounts the love story of Krishna and the beautiful maiden Radha. As Radha "enters the mystic home of her only beloved" she "musically sounds the rings of her anklets and the bells of her zone." Krishna greets her with the words: "Thy tinkling waist bells yield music almost equal to the melody of thy voice."

Much mystery relative to the spiritual life of India has been woven into legends connected with the life and activities of Krishna. These have, in turn, been interpreted in the language of both music and the dance. Also like the *Song of Solomon*, the lovely Indian song is a chant of the Mystic Marriage, voicing the soul ecstasy attendant upon divine at-one-ment. The musical bells mentioned so often in this song have reference to the harmony that continually sounds forth from an illumined soul. The rhythm of a disciple's keynote must always be attuned to that of his teacher and the particular Ray to which the latter is attuned.

All of India's religions unite on one fundamental belief:

the doctrine of the Trinity. The three aspects under which their God manifests are the Creator, the Preserver and the Destroyer. The Destroyer aspect denotes the processes of death, whereby forms that are no longer adequate or useful are disintegrated to give place to new and better forms.

The music of a nation is inseparable from the basic content of the inner life of its people. Thus, it is in accordance with nature's inner harmonies that the earliest music of India possesses a threefold rhythm. According to their theory, the three most important notes are the *graba* or opening note, the *amsa* or predominant note, and the *nyasa* or final note of a melody or *raga*, as the arrangement of sounds within the octave is called. The *amsa* or second note is now considered the most important one of the scale and is, therefore, referred to as the "soul of the raga." The beginning note correlates with the Creator aspect of the threefold Godhead, the Father principle. The second note carries the Preserver or Cosmic Christ principle. The third and final note correlates with the Destroyer or transforming principle.

It is significant that in modern Hindu music the note belonging to the Christ principle is of greatest importance and is considered the very soul of the music's measures. Unification is the keynote of the Christ impulse and the same purpose is served by music. The dominant second or Christ note in the triple-noted modern Hindu melody is, therefore, serving the evolutionary need of India today, namely, the abolishment of the caste system and a unification of the people. It may be by means of the mystic power of music that this paramount goal will be reached.

In a work entitled *The Universal History of Music,* the late Rabindranath Tagore lists the colors associated in Sanskrit with the seven musical tones. In their numerical sequence they are: black, tawny, golden, white, yellow, purple and green. Variation in the colors from those accepted by Western musicians is due to a difference in the placement and esoteric significance of the notes. While these mysteries are concealed from those who are unprepared, they are beautifully revealed to those who perceive them with spiritually opened eyes and ears.

It has been an age-long Hindu teaching that when Krishna danced celestial Beings always took part in the truly hallowed performance. When Krishna, the Sun God, is observing the annual festival of the Sun, he is depicted as playing a flute while surrounded by dancing nymphs, each one bearing a musical instrument. In this ceremonial is to be found the origin of a dance patterned after the rotation of the planets around the solar orb.

The East Indian people believe that each of the five arts was a direct revelation from the gods who gave them to man through the Vedas. Furthermore, they teach that a particularly lofty mission is assigned to music and the dance in that they have power to raise man above and beyond worldly interests and into perfect union with the Divine. The decline suffered by all the arts, whether of the East or the West, during the course of centuries bears testimony to the decadence into which civilization has fallen. In India the arts are partially asleep, as it were, awaiting a resurgence of the Spirit of the Orient to bring them again into vibrant creative expression.

No country is richer in its heritage of folk music than India. It is a direct emanation from the soul of the people. Being a Capricorn country, India's inhabitants are strongly dominated by Saturnian characteristics. These may be described briefly as outward reserve and caution but inward fiery spiritual ardor. This Saturnian influence permeates all their music. To Western ears it is strange and weird, altogether uninteresting and montonous. But when more familiar with it, an occidental listener learns to appreciate the "Saturnian drone" at its true value. This drone is an indispensible part of their music, expressing as it does the plaintive mood and soul-sorrow of a people who sense the discrepancy between their spiritual knowing and its ineffectual expression, individually and nationally.

Among the most popular of Hindu instruments are the *vina* and the *sitar,* which resemble our guitar and banjo, respectively. Both these instruments have "drone strings," though the drone is played most effectively upon two drums when tuned an octave apart.

Since the soul of India is so closely attuned to realms of the spirit, the occult power of music is inevitably accentuated. Early Indian music possessed potent healing powers and, according to legend, was also used for taming wild animals and to effect natural phenomena such as bringing rain to the crops.

The Indo-Aryan elements of music are said to have their origin in the first Vedic hymns. The *Rig Veda* (1400 B.C.) was formerly chanted in three tones. A regular system of notation was in use several centuries before the Christian Era. In it the seven notes are designated by the seven initial letters of the alphabet. This system of notation passed from the Brahmans into Persia and Arabia, and then into Europe.

There is an Indian legend to the effect that music and its allied art, the dance, were given to man by the God Siva. The cosmic dance of Siva typifies the power of rhythm in its evolutionary aspect; and in its personal aspect it relates to forces centered in the heart which, when sufficiently elevated, release the soul from the illusions of the material world.

MUSIC OF EGYPT

Music, once admitted to the soul, becomes a sort of spirit, and never dies. It wanders perturbedly through the halls and galleries of the memory, and is often heard again, distinct and living, as when it first displaced the wavelets of the air.—*Bulwer*

Music is the fourth great material want of our nature — first food, then raiment, then shelter, then music.—*Bovee*

As one thinks of the ancient land of Egypt, the lovely lines by Leigh Hunt come to mind as expressing something of its mystery and enchantment: "The Nile flows through old hushed Egypt and its sands like some grave thought threading a mighty dream."

In these studies of the ancient origins of music the aim is to trace the close correspondence that always exists between the musical and spiritual development of a people. Invariably the "Golden Age" of any nation will be the time when musical appreciation and spiritual realization

[52]

reach their highest. History indicates that the two rise and fall together.

When Egypt was in her full flowering under the Hyksos or Shepherd Kings, her music attained to great heights as both an art and a science. Much of this wisdom she bequeathed to succeeding civilizations. Ancient Greece, for example, drew upon it — as Plato indicates by his statement referring to the marvelous knowledge of the Egyptians concerning music: "The plan we have been laying down for youth was well known in Egypt. Namely, nothing but beautiful forms and fine music should be permitted in the assemblies of young people." The noted historian Strabo stated that it was required by law that children of the Egyptians be taught letters and songs together with a certain "species of music" established by the government. Requisite qualifications for the priesthood were medicine (astrological), ability to play upon stringed instruments, and worthiness to be initiated into spiritual mysteries.

The Egyptians were devout worshipers of a dual Godhead, the masculine and feminine principles as represented by Osiris and Isis, the Sun and the Moon respectively, and by the two upright columns of their Temples. The two columns of Masonry, Jachin and Boaz, can be traced to its origin. The most famous of the world's initiatory Temples are the Great Pyramid and the Sphinx, which again represent the masculine and the feminine polarities in manifestation.

In every country music has been a spontaneous growth born of the spiritual needs of the people and the religious beliefs representing them. In evidence of this, it is interesting to observe that the first known Egyptian musical instrument was the *dichord,* an instrument with two strings that was sacred to Temple use. Another instrument of this early period was a double flute consisting of two slender magic wands that were played simultaneously as an accompaniment to the Temple hymns used when a disciple was to solemnize the mystic Rite of Polarity, the uniting of the masculine and feminine principles within himself. Its rhythm, when merged with certain other rhythms, had power to further this union. Herein was the origin of modern wedding music. Wagner, music-prophet of the future, wrote the *Lohengrin* wedding music for the same purpose, so it is keyed to the initiatory Rite of Polarity, also known as the Rite of the Mystic Marriage.

A fascinating picture of the double flute was taken from a tomb in Thebes, Egypt's oldest city. The ancients always regarded death as the preserver of life. The pictured figure represents a priest dressed for an initiatory ceremonial and playing the two-pipe flute. Upon his back is a flowering vine that reaches upward and crowns his head with a halo of blossoms — obviously a tracing of the path of the fire-mist up the spine, with an attendant expansion of the spiritual flower-centers as the flame reaches the pineal and pituitary glands. A lovely old poem describes this mystic attainment as being "sweeter than honey and better than wine."

In the belief of the Egyptians, their next spiritual unfoldment was associated with Thoth or Hermes Trismegistus, the Mercury of Egypt. It was an expansion of consciousness, *three* now becoming the sacred number. Hence, not two but three deities were worshiped, Hermes being added to Osiris and Isis, Mercury to the Sun and Moon. Thus the masculine and feminine principles were augmented to complete their concept of the Holy Trinity.

Historians state that Hermes was endowed with extraordinary talents for everything conducive to the good of mankind. Out of the rude, primitive dialects of the time he fashioned a regular and symmetrical language by which he communicated to his people the first principles of astronomy. Clement of Alexandria mentions a series of books by Hermes, two on music and four on astronomy, kindred subjects of scientific instruction given in all Mystery Schools.

And he invented a lyre to which he gave three strings that produced three variations of sound: *grave, mean* and *acute. Grave* correlated to winter, *mean* to spring, *acute* to the summer. These three tones were used to assist in the evolution of the three soul-powers of man, powers known in modern terminology as the Will, Wisdom and

[54]

Activity aspects of the Godhead. The third tones played directly upon man's astral or desire body, purifying and uplifting it. Initiatory rites of the three sacred seasons were designed to bring these three soul-powers into full manifestation in the life of an aspirant to the Mysteries. Music for the ritual was played upon the *trichord,* the three-stringed lyre of Hermes, the Thrice Illustrious, whose rites were known as the Degrees of Apprentice, Fellowship and Master. These Degrees contained fundamental precepts that have been elaborated upon to form the Nine Lesser Mysteries and the thirty-three Degrees of modern Masonry.

The harp, however, appears to have held first place in Egyptian music. Even the successive shapes and styles of this instrument were an indication of the growth and decadence of that civilization. At its crudest it was bow-shaped, had only one string, and the musician had to hold it in his arms. As their civilization advanced their harp was improved and enlarged to three, four, and then seven strings; also, the base was given its present triangular shape. During the reign of Rameses III, who is generally known as the Pharaoh who reigned when the exodus of the Hebrews took place, and in the time of the Twentieth Dynasty which saw a flowering of Egyptian civilization, the harp became the royal instrument of priests and kings. Only those who had attained the dignity and rank of "holiness" were deemed worthy to play this sacred instrument within the Temples.

The framework of royal harps was of gold and ivory, inlaid with pearl and decorated with figures of gods and goddesses. Ofttimes they had as many as twenty-one strings, three times the seven dedicated to the seven planetary deities. Under the manipulation of "the minstrels of the gods," the music was of rare potency. "Musical medicine" was an actuality. Healing, along with numerous other so-called "supernatural feats," was attributed to the occult powers of this art. Temple musicians assumed a kneeling posture when playing the sacred harps for the purpose of performing magic.

The degeneration of both music and science began

with the conquest and occupation of Egypt by the Persians. As the spiritual potency of the harp waned and was forgotten, the instrument was denied its former beauty and delicacy of structure. With the nation's full decadence the "royal harp" was back to its clumsy, primitive form.

Percussion instruments work upon man's desire nature by influencing his emotional centers. Hence, they became an important factor in the martial music of Egypt. Various drums and tambourines, similar to those in current use, had a conspicuous place in her military bands. A small instrument, much like Spanish castanets and called a *sistrum,* was also popular. To it was ascribed special power for driving away evil entities. Even the sinister forces engendered by Typhon could be dissipated by it. Practically all religions assign to bells the same efficacy in attracting the intercession of guardian deities and in driving away negative influences.

According to existing records, the Egyptian priesthood also dedicated "the most sacred seven sounds" to the seven planetary bodies. Great importance was attached to the utterance of these sounds, done by the human voice only, as a means of making contact with the planetary deities and thus creating channels through which celestial Beings could transmit power to earthly worshipers. Christian Fathers later incorporated the seven tones into some of their ritual chants, such as "I am the great indestructible lyre of the whole world" and "The seven sounding tones praise Thee, the great God, the ceaseless working Father of the whole universe."

So far we have traced evolutionary development, spiritually and musically, in its relation to the Sacred Trinity. Now let us consider it in relation to the people of Egypt. The Egyptians looked upon man as a trichordal being. In addition to his visible physical form was his invisible double, the *ka* or vital body. Then there was his twofold soul, *bi,* the masculine and *ba* the feminine, and the *khoo* or luminous spark of spirit-fire. This spirit-fire contained the three principles previously described. Herein we find the uniting of the *three* and the *four,* union of the Trine with the Square which produces the power-number *seven,* sacred to all peoples and to all philosophies.

The Temple music of early Egypt appears to have been of a quiet and soothing nature. In the interval between 1700 and 1500 B.C. a more clangorous type of an accelerated tempo was introduced and was appropriately designated as "new music." History apparently repeats itself musically as well as otherwise. The "new music" was accepted and proclaimed by the masses, whereupon there resulted a division in the musical life of the people. While the masses gradually lost all knowledge of the healing and spiritual powers resident in harmony and rhythm, Temple priests and their acolytes investigated more deeply into the secrets of musical science. As Plato observed, only *good* music, according to the judgment of the priests, was taught to Egyptian youths.

During the Reign of Ramesis II (570-526 B.C.) there was a brief resurgence of recognition and understanding relative to the power and true significance of music. Then, with the final dissipation of this knowledge, occult secrets connected with tone and harmony were lost to all but the Illuminati. They became, instead, the divine heritage of the Greeks.

THE MUSIC OF GREECE

The octave formed a circle and gave our noble earth its form.
—*Pythagoras*

Music is a moral law. It gives a soul to the universe, wings to the mind, flight to the imagination, a charm to sadness, gaiety and life to everything. It is the essence of order, and leads to all that is good and just and beautiful.—*Plato*

Originally, music was given by the initiate priesthood. It was based upon the movement of the stars and was a transcription of the Music of the Spheres. According to a famous treatise written by Martianus Capella, who lived in the fifth century of our Christian era, the science of early music was divided into seven parts, namely, sounds, intervals, systems, genera, modes, mutations and melapaeia (melody). To these seven parts were added five others: rhythm, metre, organic art (instrumental art), hypocritic art (gesture) and poetic art (composition of verse).

The predominance of *five* and *seven* and their correlation with the operations of the twelve zodiacal Hierarchies had been previously noted. Five of these Hierarchies worked with nascent humanity. By reason of their great spiritual attainment they have passed into liberation beyond the earthly ken of men. The remaining seven continue to aid in man's evolutionary development. This fact is given a beautiful and symbolical interpretation in the musical staff of five lines and seven notes. The five lines are indicative of the five Hierarchies, the signs from Aries through Leo, that have attained liberation and passed on into cosmic spheres. The seven notes are representative of the signs from Virgo through Pisces, the Hierarchies working with our human life wave.

According to Aristoxenus, one of the most ancient of musical historians (40 B.C.), the contemporary Greek scale extended two octaves. We have already traced music from the time when a flute possessed fewer apertures than now and when a lyre had but three strings. The Greek system, however, was composed of five tetrachords — that is, five chords of four sounds each — with one added at the bottom of the scale to complete the double octave. Its emphasis lay in the several series of four sounds correlated with the four divine elements of Fire, Air, Earth and Water, elements out of which all physical things are created. Hence, the fourth was the favorite and most important interval. They also used four monosyllables ending in vowels as voice exercises.

Grecian musical sages knew that all phenomena was formed and controlled through a basic keynote, called by them the *mese*. Euclid stated that the *mese* was the sound whereby all other sounds were regulated. In naming and numbering their scales, the Greeks went towards the *mese* and ended with it. Their musical notes were expressed by the letters of their alphabet. The *mese* or keynote was always written as *omega*, the last letter of the alphabet and, therefore, signifying totality. Aristotle said that the *mese* was leader and sole ruler of the scale.

In modern music the genera are but two, the diatonic and the chromatic. Ancient music included a third, the enuarmonic. Each genera had some particularly characteristic tones and others that were common to the other two. Special powers were ascribed to each genera. Aristides, in the second century A.D., wrote: "The diatonic scale is manly and austere (masculine). The chromatic, sweet and pathetic (feminine). The enharmonic, animating and mild, is unifying." This is another evidence of the threefold working of the Godhead manifest in man as attributes of the Trinity, and effecting a musical influence upon his body, mind and spirit.

The mode in ancient music was equivalent to the key of modern music. Pliny names the three principal modes as Dorian, Phrygian and Lydian. Other writers have added the Aeolian and Ionian. Heraclites, a contemporary of Plato, described the Dorian mode as grave and magnificent, but severe and vehement. It was employed in martial airs. The Aeolian, grand and pompous though soothing, was used for the reception of guests and for the breaking of horses. The Ionian was austere but with a degree of elevation, force and energy. The Phrygian was consecrated to ceremonials of the Mysteries. He added that due to the subversion of all things by men, the original and specific qualities belonging to each mode had been lost. Pythagoras termed rhythm as of masculine potency and melody as feminine in power, just as we have previously ascribed rhythm to the physical body and melody to the soul.

Included in a volume containing *Phoenomena,* the famous astrological poem by Aratus — an English translation of which was published in Oxford in 1672 — are three Greek poems in the Phrygian mode belonging to the Mysteries. These poems were first given to the public in Florence in 1581 by the father of Galileo. The most important of the three is Pindar's magnificent *Hymn to Apollo.*

The majority of Greek tragedies were written by Initiates and hold a key to some phase of Initiation. Sophocles was a native of Eleusis and in early youth became a communicant of the Mysteries enacted in this sacred center. Music played an important part in preparing a candidate and in the ceremonial itself. In those ancient times poetry, music and the Mysteries were inseparable. The great tragedies, for instance, presented various aspects of Temple wisdom. Their enactment was accompanied by seven choruses depicting, by means of song and dance, the movements of the stars whereto the high festivals were geared. In the words of Cicero, music was "the foundation of all the sciences and . . . the education of children was begun by it from the persuasion that nothing could be expected of a man who was ignorant of music."

In Grecian Temples music and poetry were correlated for mystic purposes, each poetic line being accompanied by its proper musical note. A fragment of the *Hymn to Apollo* is a good example of this. Apollo ceremonials were performed to the accompaniment of a flute. He was the first to combine the healing efficacy of music and poetry and thus became the healer and the God of Physic. His most sumptuous Temple was the huge oval structure erected at Delos, where hundreds of musicians every day sang his praises and demonstrated the power of music to affect weather conditions, the growing of plants and the flow of streams. Outstanding among these musicians were the priestesses (nuns) of the Order of St. Apollo of Delos.

Amphion, who erected the first Temple to the Grecian Mercury, was invested by that god with superhuman powers relative to both music and masonry. He was able to fortify the city of Thebes, to repel invasion, and to banish all destructive influences by the magic powers of his lyre. The musical prowess of Orpheus was varied. Foremost was a species of magic known as evocation of the manes (materialization of discarnates) in Temples dedicated to this purpose. The extension of the tetrachord into the heptachord, the seven-stringed lyre, is ascribed to Orpheus, whose descent into hell to rescue Eurydice, his wife, outlines the Path of Initiation as observed in the most famous of all Grecian Temples, the Temple of Eleusis. This innovation was prompted by the fact that the time had come when, under the influence of the sevenfold planetary system, the process of awakening the seven

centers in man's vital body could begin. Hence the poet's
lines:

> The tetrachord's restraint we now despise,
> The seven-string lyre a nobler strain supplies.

The legendary goddess, Minerva, to whom all Greece
paid such high tribute, was the glorious Archangel who
became the guardian spirit of the nation. A pronounced
feminine influence was essential for the development of
the arts to the high degree they attained during its Golden
Age. Owing to Minerva's predominance, women excelled
in the arts as, perhaps, in no other land. Sappho was one
of the most exquisite of all musician-poets. Invention of
the Sapphic lyric measure is attributed to her. One of her
young disciples was the rarely gifted Corinna, whose early
death deprived the world of the full fruitage of her
splendid genius. While she was yet in her teens distin-
guished persons came from near and far to pay homage
to her accomplishments and to study with her. In the
renowned music and poetry contests, so universal in Greece
at that time, Corinna vanquished the celebrated Pindar
no less than five times in succession.

Homer wrote in his *Hymn to Apollo*: "By turns the
nine delight to sing." These lines refer to the nine Muses
so prominent in Grecian legends as the nine maidens who
presided over the arts and sciences. To the Wise they
typify the nine steps of the Mysteries. Study of the arts
and sciences were part of the initiatory regimen of the
time, and the Muses were representative of celestial Beings
who presided over the Lesser Mysteries.

To the Greeks music had a threefold purpose: to pro-
mote civilization and to humanize man; to excite or repress
passions; to serve as a remedial agent. Plutarch stated
that the supreme function of music was to praise the gods
and to educate the youth. He added that in the religious
ceremonials of the Greeks "they sang hymns to the Gods
and canticles in praise of great and good men."

Every note of Grecian music has a distinct moral and
emotional character. Following are the seven principal
keys or modes:

Mixo-Lydian — plaintive, tragic; invented by Sappho.

Lydian — low-pitched, self-indulgent, funeral music; the *Orestes* of Euripides is done in this key. The oldest fragment of Grecian music extant is the Lydian.

Phrygian — temperance.

Dorian — courage, dignity, grandeur. In the Dorian mode are the *Hymns to Dionysus, Apollo, and Callippe*.

Hypo-Lydian — *hypo* means that a key is lower by a fourth than the original key to which it is conjoined.

Hypo-Dorian — hospitable, chivalrous; approximates to the modern Minor mode.

Hypo-Phrygian — this most closely approximates to the modern Major mode; the *Hymn to Nemesis* is in the Hypo-Phrygian mode.

At a later time *hyper* was added to designate the fourth higher (sub-dominant). Gradually this music was expanded to the idea of a key for every semi-tone in the octave. Thus was formulated the system of thirteen keys.

It will be noted that, from the viewpoint of the hidden power of music as employed in the Mysteries to aid in the regeneration and illumination of the neophyte, the Phrygian and Dorian modes were most important for training and guidance. Dorian was the expressed preference of Plato. In his ideal republic he would have permitted these two modes only. The flute was especially a Phrygian instrument and as such is often mentioned by Aristotle.

Music Initiations had their share in the great contests known as the Panathenaia, the Olympia, the Pythia and the Karneia. These lovely artistic festivals were revived in medieval times in the musical contests of troubadours and Master Singers. Primarily, such song fests were concerned not with personal love and passion, but with the high and holy things of spirit.

The Greeks accounted physical prowess as of supreme importance even in musical and poetic contests since it was said that only perfect bodies were worthy to be brought into the presence of the gods by those who were to receive the mystic rites. Initiatory music was heard only in Temple rites because it carried the vibratory rhythms of other worlds and of a life beyond the mortal. The most sublime of all music is thus fittingly described: "It seemed as though it would go on forever, there was no end — only pause in a divine expectancy."

Chapter IV

CHRISTIAN ORIGINS

EARLY CHRISTIAN MUSIC

But God has a few of us whom he whispers in the ear;
The rest may reason and welcome: 'tis we musicians know.
—Abt Vogler by Robert Browning

It was customary, on some occasions, to dance round the altars whilst they sang the sacred hymns, which consisted of three stanzas or parts; The first of which, called strophe, was sung in turning from east to west; the other, named antistrophe, in returning from west to east: Then they stood before the altar, and sung the epode, which was the last part of the song.
—Archbishop John Potter

WHEN THE CHRIST impulse centered itself in the earthly globe two thousand years ago it added wings to the spirit of music. It was then impregnated with a fresh and nobler rhythm that has not as yet come into maturity, but will reach a glorious culmination during the Aquarian Age.

"New Songs" of the early Christian church were keyed to the alleluia cadences which presaged a world redeemed and a humanity emancipated. Such is the rhythm of the Planetary Christ song sounding continuously throughout the realms of earth. Much of the music used in the Christian community of that period was attuned to some high spiritual event, so the impact of these occurrences was disseminated many times over.

The Master taught His disciples the esoteric meaning and purpose of sound and rhythm. His most profound teaching, given at the time of the Last Supper, was climaxed with a Glory Hymn of Initiation such as St. Paul refers to in I Corinthians 14:15: "I will pray with the spirit, and I will pray with the understanding also; I will sing with the spirit, and I will sing with the understanding also."

Philo refers to the nocturnal vigils of the first Christian saints, or Initiates, numbered among his Therapeutae, as

[64]

follows: "After supper their sacred songs began. When
all were risen they selected from the rest two choirs, one
of men and one of women, and from each of these a person
of majestic form and well skilled in music to lead the
band. They chanted hymns in honor of God, composed in
different measures and modulations, now singing together
and then answering each other by turns."

In this musical ceremonial we observe the influence of
inner-plane Temple ritual. Many disciples of the Mystery
Schools have brought back into waking consciousness,
usually in that mystic hour just before dawn, a memory of
Temple ceremonials in which rhythmic chanting stirred
the soul to its depths. Blending of the masculine and feminine in sound reflects the blending of the positive and
negative forces for the accomplishment of definite initiatory work upon the body of an aspirant or upon the psychic
envelope of the earth planet. The pulsations of rhythm
are accompanied by a complex pattern of sound which
becomes actually visible to spiritual vision as ethereal structures, more or less durable according to the endurance of
the tones which create them. These are experienced by
the awakened one as an actual temple whose walls are
harmony vibrating to a distant keynote. In architecture
these subtle rhythms are made visible in masculine lines
and spires and feminine arches and domes, features characteristic of some of the most beautiful cathedrals. It was
St. Ignatius, a disciple of St. John, who introduced the
Music Ritual into the churches of his day, proclaiming this
to be the true angelic method of praising God in song.

The oldest known Christian hymn-text, the *Hymn of
the Saviour,* is attributed to Clement of Alexandria, famous
leader of the Christian School in Egypt said to have been
founded by St. Mark. Clement's equally famous disciple,
Origen, described in beautiful symbology the effects of the
various musical instruments. The trumpet, he said, represents the Word (power of intonation) ; the drum is effica-
cious in the destruction of base passions (it correlates with
man's desire body which is powerfully influenced by rhythm
both for good and ill) ; stringed instruments voice the cry
of the eager soul enamored of Christ.

indebted to Eusebius, Bishop of Caesarea in
alestine, for the most detailed account of the
and customs of the Therapeutae of Egypt, who correspond to the Essenes of Palestine among whom Joseph,
Mary and Jesus were numbered. Eusebius states that in
the assemblies of the Therapeutae the Psalms were not
recited but sung in certain melodious tones. St. Basil, his
successor, composed the liturgy which bears his name and
is still used in Eastern churches.

It was St. Ambrose who is said to have introduced into
the Church the diatonic scale of Pythagoras. Pythagoras
has been termed the father of Western music, and he was
the first to associate numbers (vibration) with music. The
Ambrosian chant is an outstanding example of the music
considered essential by the School of Christian Initiation.
The angelic hymn, *Gloria in Excelsis Deo,* was the song
by which a neophyte was lifted into communion with angelic
beings. Two hundred years after Ambrose (Bishop of
Milan 378-394 A.D.), St. Gregory gave alphabetical
names to the tones of the scale, namely, A, B, C, D, E, F,
and G.

The prime objective of all initiatory music in the Temples of antiquity was to bring about physical purification,
and renewal, mental stimulation and alertness, spiritual
exhilaration and illumination. In the coming New Age
this will once more be the glorious mission of music and
musicians.

In 590 A.D., in the very opening century of the Piscean
Age, Pope Gregory changed the initial rhythms of Christian initiatory music. At that time the Church was becoming increasingly unresponsive to the spiritual outpourings
which Christ had loosed upon the earth, and which had
inspired and illumined the earliest Christians. A change
in the music was necessary to meet this negative trend.
Since then the Gregorian Chant has been the basis of
religious music in the Western World. Bach, Mozart and
other great music masters retained these Gregorian measures. While the chant of Gregory still lives, his antiphonary
or initiatory music ritual has been lost due to the further
descent of the Church into materiality.

In A.D. 596 Gregory sent St. Augustine to teach the Saxons mathematics, astronomy and music "in the manner of the early church." St. Augustine was deeply impressed with the music of the barbarians which, to his ear, possessed an unearthly beauty — a hint of the great music destined to appear later in Northern Europe.

Mention has been made earlier of the correlation between instruments of seven strings and the seven planets, the seven body centers of man, and so on. They have a like correlation with the seven vowels of the alphabet. Anyone exploring the history of music would come near to occult truth in a surmise that herein is to be found the origin of Christian chants. According to Hebrew tradition, the vowels were too sacred to be committed to writing. Like the Phoenician alphabet, transmitted to the Greeks by the legendary Cadmus, the Hebrew alphabet lacked vowels.

In India the seven vowels are recognized as seven phases of Brahma while the other letters of the alphabet are regarded as representative of forces from which the universe emanated. The Hindus also realize the importance of vowel sounds in esoteric unfoldment. Their sacred mantra are among the finest examples of what we may call magical verse. Similarly, the Lost Word of the Old Testament of the Hebrews, which is the Name of God, consisted of the chanting of a series of vowel sounds in a special order, as it is known was also done in the Temples of Egypt. The Hebrew Scriptures are full of sacred mantra which are not commonly recognized as such.

Every Mystery School has its own method of development suited to the needs of the souls entrusted to its care. Although all Schools are centered in one fundamental truth and are organized on the same basic pattern, there are variations according to the evolutionary requirements of the egos comprising the student body. The early Christian Church was no exception to this rule. Its music was brought through "by means of angelic vision," as it was so beautifully described at the time. In other words, it was under the direction of inner-plane Teachers, such as imaged in the Greek Orpheus who was taken by the Christians as a symbol of their Christ.

The ancients, who well understood the power and magic of music, realized that the musical keynote of a composition was of primary importance, for it was by means of this keynote that a musical composition was united with vital centers of power in inner realms; and that the force from such centers was disseminated by means of the music in accord with them. It has been stated that the first Mass written by Pope Gregory was attuned to the musical keynote of the Angel Song heard by shepherds in the hills near Bethlehem on the night of the Nativity.

Dissonances were also incorporated into certain secular compositions. The Church Fathers of those days called them "devil notes" because dissonant tones produced a sinister Mephistophelean effect. Church music was carefully guarded against this disruptive influence. Hence, the music of the early Church was much the same as music used in Temples of Greece and Egypt when the Mysteries were celebrated.

There are three principal receiving centers in the human body. One of these is at the base of the spine; a second is at the heart; the third is located at the upper forefront of the head. Those original chants were so composed as to impinge directly upon these three centers, designated by contemporary writers as "flowers." The motif of the Gregorian Chant has been described as "a musical arch, rising, pausing at the topmost span, and then descending."

The sacred ministry of music had been all but submerged in the wave of dense materialism which has engulfed the world since the beginning of the fifteenth century. Bach, Beethoven and Wagner have been the brightest musical lights since that time, and great honor must be accorded them for their part in keeping alive the spiritual significance of music.

St. Augustine wrote eloquently of the manner in which music led him toward the truth. His famous work, *De Musica,* has been accounted the first Christian treatise to deal with the psychology of music. In it he also treats of various other phases of esoteric music, such as meter and versification which have to do with the power of rhythm. Poets know that every inspired thought enters the consciousness in a rhythm peculiar to itself, like the heartbeat of an unborn child. St. Augustine refers to the spiritual and eternal meaning of numbers, wherein the true science of music has its immutable foundation. The *Song of Sibyl,* an acrostic of twenty-seven lines on the Greek word *Ichthus* meaning fish, and used as referring to the "fisher of men," the Lord Christ, is recorded by St. Augustine. The following lines are representative:

> Behold the King shall come through the ages,
> Sent to be here in the flesh and judge at the last of the world.

INTONING THE BIBLE

Music is well said to be the speech of angels.—Carlyle

Music is the child of prayer, the companion of religion.—Chateaubriand

Though the Bible is the world's most popular printed work, there are nevertheless more home Bible phonograph records than there are printed versions. Most of the Bible was originally composed to be read *aloud* as a liturgical exercise, and the old prophets and priests who first intoned it in Hebrew were trained musicians.

The present Jewish sacred service derives its strangely moving music from the original songs and admonitions of the prophets, while most of the popular King James version of the Bible was translated from Hebrew to Greek to Latin, and then to English. Much of the music must have been lost on the way, but the sonorous delivery of the ceremonial phrases gains a new respect for the English language.—*The Woman*

The above interesting excerpt is taken from the *Woman's Digest.* When mankind, due to his deepening involvement in materiality, practically lost knowledge of the hidden power of music, he also lost knowledge of the power of intonation. During the New Age the occult power and magic of music will be recovered and then the use of intonation will become more general. David and Solomon, two of the most illumined teachers of the Old Testament Dispensation, wrote both the Psalms and Ecclesiastes for intonation, and only in this way are their high spiritual potencies revealed.

The magic of the Church is concealed in the Mass, and the efficacy of the Mass is concealed in its intonation or chanting. Early Masses were composed by musicians who understood this inner power — musicians such as Ambrose, Palestrina and, later, Bach. They were most careful to select the proper keynote to which each of the Masses was attuned.

In the Golden Age of Greece there were many poetry contests in which the reading was always to an accompaniment of music. This music sounded the keynote of the reader, or of the current month, or of the day on which the contest was held — for the days of the week are correlated to the planets of our solar system. The keynote of each planet sounds one of the seven notes of the diatonic scale. As the stellar orbs circle about the Sun, their tones in unison are incorporated into the glory song called the Music of the Spheres.

From birth to death every individual continually sounds his own musical keynote. This note is located in the nerve cells of the cerebellum (feminine brain center) which lies at the back of the skull. Few persons are sufficiently sensitized to hear their own keynote. Some, however, are intuitive enough to recognize it and have even accompanied their prayers and meditations by musical compositions written in that key.

In the New Age music will become an increasingly important factor in education. Tiny children will be taught to intone nursery rhymes to music sounding the keynote of the day or of the current month; or, if the instruction be individual, to the keynote of the child's own natal sign.

As already noted, healing groups, twelve in number representing the twelve zodiacal signs, will treat ailments according to the natal signs of patients, and the work will be done to music keyed to the current month. If any individual of the group does individual work he will use the keynote of his own particular sign. By this healing practice — a science well understood by the early Egyptian priesthood and used by them in the Mysteries, and also used by Pythagoras — miraculous results will be accomplished for those suffering physically, mentally or spiritually.

An eastern Master, known as The Tibetan, wrote the

following concerning the powers of color and music in the New Age:

The Mysteries will restore color and music as they essentially are to the world and do it in such a manner that the creative art of today will be to this new creative art what a child's building of wooden blocks is to a great cathedral such as Durham or Milan.

When the magical powers of sound are rediscovered and scientifically directed to a specific purpose, such, for instance, as healing, no more potent passages for intonation will be found anywhere than in the Bible. Among these may be mentioned especially some contained in the Old Testament Song of Songs, Ecclesiastes, and Psalms and the first chapter of the Gospel of St. John. When man has learned how to release the mantramic powers embodied in such inspired utterances, he will be master of energies transcending even those unleashed by the atomic physicist of today. They will be energies of yet another and higher dimension.

MEDIEVAL MUSIC

Some of the Fathers went so far as to esteem the love of music a sign of predestination, as a thing divine, and reserved for the felicities of heaven itself.—*Sir William Temple*

In this era of dense materialism it is difficult to comprehend the power which music exerted upon the medieval mind when it was an essential element in the life of the people. Their music was not our music; but such as it was, it entered into every waking moment of the life, and even into dreams.

Christmas and Easter have long been the highlights of the Christian world. The most important music is built around these two holy festivals. In our *New Age Bible Interpretation* series it has been stated frequently that the early Christian Church was a School of Initiation wherein was taught the glorious Christ Mysteries. This fact was well known by the Apostles, and also by the early Christian Fathers who attested to it many times. The Christmas season celebrates the birth of Jesus, bearer of the Lord Christ, while the Easter season commemorates His resurrection. Upon the initiatory Path Christmas is indicative of the birth of the Christ within man himself while Easter symbolizes liberation of man's spirit from his body at will, this attainment being through Initiation. The human body is then no longer a prison-house, but an entrance gate, leading to grander and broader service. St. Paul was referring to such development when he said: "I knew a man in Christ above fourteen years ago, (whether in the body, I cannot tell; or whether out of the body, I cannot tell: God knoweth); such an one caught up into the Third Heaven; how that he was caught up into paradise, and heard unspeakable words, which it is not lawful for man to utter."

The Advent season that precedes Christmas and the Lenten Season that precedes Easter are periods of intensive preparation for these high events. Of course the actual work of preparation varies from individual to individual; but all alike have the extra help of the inpouring cosmic forces which cause the entire planet to vibrate like a bell at these holy seasons. Musicians who are spiritually attuned to planetary rhythms do actually convey the celestial music to earth, as we have said; and in the Middle Ages a very definite kind of music was provided to aid disciples in making their preparation for the high planetary festivals.

The Christmas and Easter rites are repeated each year in the Christian Mystery Temple located in the etheric realms. Persons still living on earth today have witnessed these sublime events, which are led by the blessed Lord Christ Himself. Some neophytes are observers only, but many have their part in the inner-plane rituals. These are not mere dramatic spectacles in which the neophytes play their parts; but they are, in a sense, the archetypes of earthly dramas. The neophyte does truly live the Christ Mystery in his person, to the accompaniment of the music of celestial choirs who behold him as he is in the eyes of God, Virgin Spirit, pure and perfect in every particular. For a brief moment he KNOWS HIMSELF AS A DIVINE BEING, sustained in this understanding by the Hierophants and celestial Hierarchies; and sometimes he will remember on the next day what has happened. But even if he does not remember, the healing virtue of the cosmic ceremonial remains with him forevermore, slowly purifying and refining the outer man. Nor are these neophytes the only beneficiaries. The whole earth globe is bathed in a pure light and there is no living being so insensate that he is not, for an instant at least, touched and uplifted by the Christ Song of this blessed festival season.

From time to time Great Ones on inner planes send an illumined music messenger to bestow upon humanity some echoings of these celestial choirs, immortal music that will live as long as the earth endures. Such music includes a number of early Christmas carols, Ave Marias, and the Passions of St. Matthew and St. John. The latter transcribe the initiatory music which accompanied the entrance of these two great saints into the glories of the Christ Mysteries. No one can listen in a spirit of reverence and devotion to the sublime Passion music without experiencing an impulse toward nobler living. In fact, the music was written and performed to hasten the upliftment of mankind during the Middle Ages.

The Lenten season is climaxed by the events of Holy Week. Music for Holy Week is attuned to the rhythm of events occurring on the successive days of that period. The brilliant processional of Palm Sunday, with its triumphant hosannas, is succeeded by the events of Monday, Tuesday and Wednesday. On Holy Thursday emphasis is laid on the footwashing, a most impressive ceremonial based on humility — one of the most important teachings given to disciples on the Path. The sweet sorrow of Good Friday and Holy Saturday is climaxed by the glorious alleluias of Easter Sunday and Easter Monday.

Physicians of the twelfth century prescribed music during the meal hours for refractory or temperamental children. Music was considered so important to young people that it held a conspicuous place in the institutional life of European orphans, and children were encouraged to develop whatever musical talent they might have. This led to the formation of children's choirs, an outstanding feature of musical activities during medieval days. The choirs would sing in their own villages and in nearby provinces; then, as their fame increased, they were taken on concert tours. A notable example of the excellent work of such children's choirs as they exist today is the splendid musicianship of the Vienna Boys' Choir which makes annual concert tours the world over, always attracting large and delighted audiences.

The troubadours and the minnesingers of the Middle Ages were servants of esoteric schools in many instances. It was for this reason that they incurred the enmity of the orthodox Church of Rome. Their supposedly sensual imagery, like that of the *Song of Solomon,* conceals esoteric doctrines of great profundity — for their so-called love songs were really soul songs addressed to the most beautiful lady (Wisdom) whose favor they sought. These singers gradually built up their own esoteric schools; and the Master Singers, who headed the ranks of the troubadours and minnesingers, were frequently high Initiates. Wolfram of Eschenbach, whose *Parsifal* was the foundation of Wagner's magnificent opera of the same title, was such a Master Singer.

The medieval musical Initiates tried, as did the Greeks, to employ music for the alleviation of human ills, physical, mental and moral. Their coming marked the appearance of bowed instruments. Their lives and their art were pure and holy, and the love songs they sang were in measures associated today with sacred music — a fact significant in itself. Many monks joined their ranks, and troubadours were honored and privileged guests of most monasteries. Verily, they were among the saints of the Middle Ages. The themes on which they were composed were largely biblical, though a later trend was more secular and philosophical.

The Schools of the Troubadours were divided into three grades: pupil, singer and Master. The latter alone was considered worthy to bring through new compositions. The Master Songs, with their strange rhythms, were accentuated at certain intervals with "flowers." These rhythms, whence originated the cadenced and stately church music of our day, impinged upon certain vital centers in the bodies of those who were sufficiently sensitive, and aided their further awakening. The Master Singer contest introduced by Wagner in *Tannhauser* pictures something of the musical initiatory ritual of that time.

The era of the troubadours may be dated as from the eleventh to the thirteenth centuries. The ordered rhythm of their music was characteristic of initiatory music in general. There was no sharp line drawn between sacred and secular music as they both dealt with every phase of human life.

In Germany the minnesingers sang the tenderest and most chivalrous songs of love, a love that is pure and holy because it is born of the soul and spirit. Most famous of these singers were Walther von der Wogelweide and Wolfram von Eschenbach, who were contemporaries. As musician-seers they took part in the Initiations by Song in the Wartburg Castle of Landgrave Hermann of Thuringia in 1207, much as portrayed by Wagner in his opera *Tannhauser*. There really was a knight-troubadour named Tannhauser who lived in that era (he is sometimes confused with another Tannhauser who lived a century or two earlier) ; and Von Eschenbach and Walther von der Wogelweide, as well as the Landgrave Hermann himself, were all notable historic characters. One of Walther's most beautiful songs was associated with the Crusade of 1228 and was written in Palestine:

> Life's true worth at last beginneth,
> Now my sinful eyes behold
> The Holy Land, the earth that winneth
> Fame for glories manifold.
> I have won my life-long prayer,
> I am in the country where
> God in human shape did fare.

Prominent among English contributors to the medieval Knighthood of Song was St. Godric (1170) whose music was dictated to him through angelic vision. It was a gift that came to him when, upon the death of his beloved sister, he implored heaven as to her welfare and was vouchsafed a vision of her with the Madonna and Angels. One of the most exalted hymns he wrote is dedicated to "Christ and Sainte Marie."

The famous *Canticle of the Sun* by St. Francis of

Assissi (1182-1226) was originally attuned to mystic rhythms — not, perhaps, through Initiation but through Francis's own spontaneous contact with the archangelic Christ. A manuscript preserved in Assissi which contains the Canticle has space also for the melody which, apparently, has been lost.

So clearly did Initiates of the Musical Ray perceive that the power of the spoken word was inseparably interwoven with the enchantment of accent and intonation that they coined a maxim: "A voice without music is a mill without water."

The Church still retains considerable knowledge of the occult powers of music. For example in the last century a Mass was composed and sung in St. Peter's for the cessation of a plague in Rome. The score contained twenty-four different parts and was sung by a choir of two hundred singers, who occupied circles in the dome. The sixth choir was placed in the summit of the cupola. This is the plan Wagner followed for the Grail Temple scenes in *Parsifal,* and we may be sure something similar was known to his great forerunner, Wolfram von Eschenbach.

Clement of Alexandria, a foremost teacher of the Christian Mysteries, significantly describes their initiatory music thus: "This is the chosen mountain of the Lord, it is dedicated to Truth. A mountain of great purity with chaste shades. It is inhabited by the daughters of God, those fair Lambs who celebrate together the *venerable orgies,* collecting the chosen Choir. The singers are holy men, their song is the hymn of the Almighty King. Virgins chant, Angels glorify, prophets discourse, while music sweetly sounding is heard."

FROM MEDIEVAL TO MODERN CHURCH MUSIC: PALESTRINA

Palestrina has been designated the father of modern church music. In him the strands of music lore from the Middle Ages draw together into a new pattern. He was born in the year 1526 in the village of Palestrina, Italy. His real name was Giovanni Pierluigi de Palestrina, but he became known to the public by the name of his birthplace.

During his life he held a number of important positions connected with the Church of Rome. In 1551 he was appointed music director of Guilia Chapel in the Vatican. Three years later he dedicated his *First Book of Masses* to the Pope. Then he became Chapelmaster in the Church of St. John Lateran, also in Rome, a post he held for five years. The next ten years he served similarly in St. Marie Maggiori. In 1564 Pope Pius IV appointed a commission of eight Cardinals to consider the improvement of church music; Palestrina was one of the composers who submitted Masses for their approval. Of the three presented by him, his Mass of Pope Marcellus II was accepted as a model of purity and style. This great composition is so majestic in beauty that it became a pattern for the music of the Roman Church. He composed ninety-three Masses in all, the beauty and type of which are still emulated by composers of sacred music.

The Oratorio

During the course of the sixteenth century Italian church music wandered so far from the chaste ideal of Palestrina as to lose almost wholly its sacred style. Innovations in the field of music brought about a conflict between the more modern mode and the old ecclesiastical style, the latter struggling in Rome to maintain its ground. The consequence was that a school of music came into existence that began to perform in the oratorium compositions relating to subjects from sacred history. Thus originated the *oratorio*.

This new school was founded by Philip de Neri, a native of Florence, Italy, now known as the father of the oratorio. De Neri was born in 1515. He was another saintly character. Even as a young man he was dubbed "good Philip" by his friends. His virtue was such that after his death he was canonized by the Roman Church. From his youth he was interested primarily in the spiritual upliftment of depraved and down-trodden fellow human beings and in the moral and spiritual education of young people. To more effectively further this project, he developed the oratorio in an endeavor to entertain young folk and to so interest them in spiritual matters as to lead them away from worldly pleasures.

The success of this musical venture in Florence of the sixteenth century was quite remarkable. A number of priests associated themselves with de Neri in this work and became known as Brothers of the Oratory. This type of music was used especially during the Lenten season, and eventually it became the custom to perform an oratory every Wednesday and Friday during Lent. Later, the oratorio spread from Italy into France; and then into England where it received, perhaps, its highest development.

Many other composers have applied their genius to this line of composition, notable among them being Haydn and Handel. Perhaps the best-known of Haydn's oratorios is *The Return of Tobias, The Seven Last Words* and, doubtless the most beautiful of them all, *Creation* with its magnificent ensembles, chorales and orchestral interludes. Handel's best-known oratorios are *Israel in Egypt* and the beloved, world-famous *Messiah,* which continues to play an important part in all Christian music festivals celebrating Christmas and Easter. The genius of Mendelssohn attained to its perfect flowering in his oratorios. The two that are heard most often are *St. Paul* and *Elijah.*

To repeat, the oratorio received its name from the oratory or chapel, a place of prayer. It serves as a bridge for connecting ancient and medieval music with modern, and occupies the place in church music that opera occupies in secular music. Oratorios are always based on some spiritual subject, usually a biblical text, *Job* and *The Prodigal Son* being great favorites.

As we have before stated, from time to time Great Ones who guide human evolution send illumined musical messengers to earth to perform some specific mission. Such a messenger was Johann Sebastian Bach (1685-1750). His mission was to unite intellect with soul. The remarkable mathematical precision of his music makes a strong appeal to the intellect while his great musical prowess tends to awaken and enhance powers of the soul. Thus, his music had a tendency to lighten in some degree the dark cloud of materialism that was rapidly enveloping the Western world.

Another notable messenger of this same period was George Frederick Handel (1685-1759). Many of these illumined musicians came to earth understanding what their mission was to be. Others were unaware of their destiny until some holy exhilaration or the exaltation of a spiritual vision revealed to them the work they were to perform. Handel was among those of this second group.

One of the greatest achievements in musical history is Handel's *Messiah*. It was the product of pure inspiration. Tenderness, purity, grandeur and an almost prophetic elevation characterize the work. Moral force and spiritual power flow from its tonal patterns. This is what Handel himself hoped for in his composition. When a friend once complimented him on his musicianship, Handel replied, "I should be sorry if I only entertained them; I wished to make them better."

THE MUSIC OF FOLKLORE

We have shown how the early Christians learned to use "angelic music" to establish communion between human beings and the celestial hosts; but it is not generally realized that the "angels" of Christian esotericism are no other than the winged gods of the so-called pagans. Ancient Etruscan tomb paintings and sculptures, for instance, show the soul being carried by a winged spirit whose head is encircled by a halo of light. Many of the Greek gods were winged. Iris, Juno's lovely messenger, who is sometimes portrayed carrying a child in her arms, was winged and enhaloed by the rainbow. The Dead Sea texts show that the words "god" and "angel" were used interchangeably in some instances by early Jewish and Christian mystics; and even Dante calls the angels "the other gods." The Book of the Secrets of Enoch declares that everything in the universe, even every blade of grass, the herbs of the field as well as the stars in heaven, has each its spirit or angel. The tiny beings dwelling invisibly among flowers and herbs, and other nature spirits, were called by the ancients the little or lesser gods. Early Christianity understood these things and so the native belief in fairies was never stamped out in Europe.

As each race of human beings is governed by an Archangel who hovers like a cloud over the land where its people dwell, so the nature spirits of that area, together with the humans who dwell there, live and breathe the spiritual atmosphere of the great Archangel; and so it is that folklore and folk music seem to express a common purpose and design, since all bear the stamp of the race spirit, and it is impossible to deal at any length with either folk literature or folk music without touching upon the realms of the nature spirits, the invisible fairy creatures who carry on their evolution alongside that of nature's visible kingdoms.

Truly one can hear the patter of tiny feet as gnomes and fairies dance and sing in Edward Grieg's *Hall of the Mountain King;* or catch a glimpse of them as they wing their way over misty mountain crags. Again, one senses the presence of water spirits dancing among the waterfalls of the North in Sibelius' *Swan of Tuonella.* The listener is similarly entranced by DeBussy's *Afternoon of a Faun,* in which the music transports one into the sylvan languor of airy beings in their innocent play. After such incursions into fairy land (which is also angel land, to a degree, for angels also move among the fairies) it is difficult to return to the affairs of the mundane world.

Another spiritually illumined music messenger was Cesar Franck (1882-1890). His inspired music seems to draw heaven closer to earth and to lift earth to heaven. Cesar Franck was a saintly individual who dedicated himself entirely to the noblest meaning and purpose of spiritual music. It is not surprising, then, that much of his inspiration was received from angelic beings. For this reason his music is deemed to possess great healing and revitalizing qualities by those engaged in the profession of music therapy.

Ottarino Respighi (1879-1936) must be mentioned as one of the most interesting modern "nature musicians" of Italy. He is justly famous for his charming compositions *The Pines of Rome, The Fountains of Rome* and *The Festivals of Rome*. In the two first named, together with his *Song of tne Birds* and numerous other compositions, he expresses the sheer natural beauty which is his native land. The third touches upon the deep mystic powers belonging to early centuries of the Latins.

Later came an innovation in music known as the "Romantic Movement." Grieg (1843-1907) represented this departure in Norway; Sibelius (1865-1958) in Finland; Debussy, in France. Much of the work of these composers is based upon folk music and folk legends. Most notable among them were Greig and Sibelius, both known as "the supreme high priests of the music of Northern Europe." However, Claude Debussy (1862-1918) is definitely included in this category. The music of these composers is descriptive of the sound of wind, the dash of waves, the roar of thunder or the rush of waterfalls. Futhermore, so closely did they live in attunement with Nature that she revealed to them the secrets of her very heart, and they were able to convey musically much of her spirit, activities and functions — secrets rarely known or recognized by modern man. In their compositions may be heard the dainty tripping of fairy feet, the rhythmic laughter of airy sprites, the delicate tones of those nymphs that inhabit the element of water. These inner secrets account for so much of their music being irresistibly fascinating, music that inspires many listeners to probe more deeply into the hidden meanings of life.

Chapter V

MUSIC OF THE AMERICAN INDIAN

PRIMITIVE TRANSMISSION OF NATURE'S HARMONIES

Indian music is like the wild flowers that have not yet come under the transforming hand of the gardener.—Selected

*A*S WE HAVE SAID, the soul of a people is revealed in its music as in no other way, for music is pure soul expression. The more primitive a race, the more clearly does it express the essential nature and quality of its innermost being in its creation of music and art forms. Representation of the beautiful is one of man's first creative activities and, consequently, it becomes a most effective medium for bodying forth the predominant characteristics of a people.

The natural sensitivity of the race as a whole is strongly marked in Indian art. For example, all forms of Indian art incorporate, in one way or another, the spirit of prayer. Their ceremonial pipe and plumed prayer sticks are symbolical of the incense of worship as it rises on the wind to the Great Spirit above. Examination in the light of spiritual science reveals that their pottery, bead work, weaving and basket designing are fairly resonant with this spirit of prayer.

Music enters into the very warp and woof of Indian life. Every event of importance in their daily round of activities is embodied in song. These songs are not merely harmonious groupings of words set to music. They constitute a blend of poetry, rhythm and tone or melody. This union is given added significance by the psychic powers focused, through centuries of reverent use, in the legends or ceremonials that form the background of the songs.

An interesting notation is from the pen of Dr. James W. Powell, one-time director of the American Bureau of Ethnology. He states that rhythm is the first element of music and he assigns rhythm to the most primitive stage

of man's development, which he terms "the hunter stage."
As man moved into a higher stage of development —
which Dr. Powell terms "the shepherd stage" — a new
element was introduced, melody. It is here that we may
discover the strange and miraculous potency frequently
observed to accompany a performance of Indian ceremonial
music, such as the rain chants of the arid Southwest and
the wonderful efficacy of their healing rituals.

Music critics assert that Indian music contains only two
elements of the musical trinity, namely, melody and
rhythm; and that their music lacks the most potent element, harmony. This is correct according to standards by
which music is generally judged. But if the subject be
analyzed esoterically, it will be found that harmony is not
altogether lacking. Harmony is there, but it is audible
only to a higher octave of etheric hearing. Anyone who is
capable of hearing the fine etheric harmonies of nature
will note how accurately many of its sounds, above and
below the ordinary range of hearing, have been incorporated into Indian music. It is this symphony of nature that
gives the unusual "other-world" atmosphere which is so
much a part of an all-Indian concert — an effect doubly
enhanced if the program is heard out-of-doors and in native
Indian surroundings. This faithful transcription of nature's
sublime harmonies, brought through by ancient Indian
seers or holy men, gives to their music its amazing healing
potency and also the auric green color which suffuses, and
emanates from all true Indian musical compositions as
they are performed. It will be remembered that Nature's
color note is green.

These inner-plane qualities, incorporated by Indian
sages into their musical productions, makes a literal transcription practically impossible. To be fully appreciated,
and estimated at their real value, they must be heard in
their natural environment. The American Indian is a
child of nature. Whoever listens to his music should not
do so out of mere curiosity or in a mood of flippantly seeking a new sensation. He should listen in a spirit of respect-
ful inquiry and reverence for the soul of the race. Then
will he come away with a greater appreciation and under-

standing of the Indian people and of Mother Nature, to which they are so closely attuned.

THE HIDDEN SIGNIFICANCE OF INDIAN MUSIC

O Great Spirit, maker of men, forbid that I judge any man until I have walked for two full moons in his moccasins.—An old Indian prayer

Music is an essential part of the Red Man's religion. His use of the art is largely for the purpose of invoking super-material powers. True to esoteric tradition, such music is generally in minors. No other music can be compared with that of the Indians for elaborateness and intricacy of rhythms. Their emotions, both joyous and sad, find fullest expression by means of song. It is the medium by which a departing friend is sent on his way and then welcomed upon his return. Songs herald the victory of warriors, the joys of marriage, the birth of an incoming soul. Weirdly fascinating are the strangely uneven minors which announce news of a warrior's defeat in battle or accompany the funeral procession of a departed chieftain. Most interesting are the rhythmic measures employed by their medicine men in their healing practice. Since time immemorial this race has made use of musical therapy. Those developing modern techniques of that science will find inestimable treasures concealed within Indian lore if they will explore it with sufficient diligence.

Of deep interest to esoteric investigators are the many Indian songs invoking the spirits of the disembodied, for music is probably the most effective means of rending the veil between the seen and the unseen. Students of music therapy are now becoming aware of this fact. It appears that Indians have always had this knowledge and have thus made use of music for countless centuries.

The Red Man has also demonstrated profound occult learning in his application of nature music. The efficacy of his rain chants is well known; also that he employs this art to increase the productivity of crops and for their protection. He has songs to invoke the spirits of fire, air, water and earth. Because of his natural clairvoyance he is able to see these ethereal beings, to comprehend something of their functions in the vast economy of nature, and to work directly with them.

We hear a great deal about the incoming Aquarian Age when art and religion will be one. Endowed with great spiritual wisdom, the *first Americans* have always understood them to be so united. They reverence God as the Great Mystery, and they are steeped in awe for that Mystery as they behold its manifestation in the beauties of nature. Since their communion with nature and nature's God is sacred, they invest natural phenomena with supernatural powers. An exquisite little song, with its otherworld over-tones, describes how a little bush is singing its song to a big tree that stands above it.

To the ordinary person this would be mere poetical imagery related to Indian mythology, but an esotericist exalts in the beautiful truth therein. He understands that the voices of nature are not poetical fancy but a literal fact, and that by means of their voices nature's children hold communion. Tree devas shed their beneficent rays upon surrounding growth. One possessing clairvoyance can see mature trees bend in blessing over their young charges which, in turn, lift their heads upward in a responsive gesture of praise and thanksgiving. Some sensitive Indian closely attuned to nature's inner and outer processes caught the tones accompanying this delicate ethereal interchange and gave it expression in his music.

Elizabeth Barrett Browning glimpsed something of this higher beauty when she sang

> Earth's crammed with heaven
> And every common bush afire with God,
> But only he who sees takes off his shoes.

The flute is the instrument favored for playing Indian music, probably because it lends itself so readily to imitating notes of nature. It holds first place in primitive Indian orchestras. Next in importance is the drum. Its premonitory muffled beat is used to sound the inevitable fate motif, a motif that gives to their sacred ceremonial chants a somewhat ominous air. The unequal rhythms occurring between the drum and the voice produce a most uncanny effect. Percussion instruments are expressive of man's lower or animalistic nature, his unleashed passions. Wind instruments, on the contrary, express the mental faculties which exert control over the lower emotions. In Indian music there is a balance between the two. Irregular drum rhythms, similar to those of the weird tom-toms of South Sea islanders, are employed with telling effect in the magical and hypnotic incantations of the Indians, whereas flutes are used with equal effectiveness in their religious ceremonials.

Legends about the origin of the flute are woven most interestingly into the mythology of various Indian tribes, thus revealing that its use has been common for long ages. A very old native gave voice to his reverence for the flute when he said, "There has always been a flute, for the flute is as old as the world."

MUSIC AND THE FEMININE INFLUENCE IN INDIAN CULTURE

Wherever a people has attained a sufficient degree of culture for it to be fundamental to their civilization, it will be noted that women hold a place of high esteem and real importance. This is especially true of the American Indian, although not widely understood. An ancient Indian maxim makes it graphically clear: "Marriage among Indians is like traveling in a canoe. The man is in front and paddles the canoe. The woman sits in the stern, but she *steers*."

Because of the exigencies of Indian life, it was long necessary for men to be absent for months at a time on warring and hunting expeditions. All tribal duties were, therefore, delegated to the women. As they became proficient in essential types of manual labor, they were honored by giving them a greater range of responsibility and usefulness. In native lore, grains (wheat and corn) were feminine in gender, and numerous agricultural tribes deputed to women the honor of planting seed. In secret ceremonials preceding planting and harvesting seasons homage was paid to the spirit of womanhood. Although it was a common practice for the males to walk in advance of their women, this was a matter of protection rather than an evidence of the latter's inferior status. Among some tribes the home was in the woman's name, and she had authority to dismiss her husband if his way of life was displeasing to her.

Children were the cementing bond between husband and wife. Our Western civilization could learn much from the red men relative to preparation for conception and birth. From early childhood they were taught the sacredness of these starred events, and the obligation of building a fine and beautiful body. Herein lies the reason why artists and sculptors find great inspiration in portraying Indian figures.

Conception was timed to occur in harmony with the heavenly orbs, and the following nine days constituted a sacred interval. The prospective mother went into a forest sanctuary for meditation and prayer, that she might attune herself to angelic Beings who would guard and protect her until the glad day of delivery. These celestial Beings were said to be attracted by music. Exquisitely ethereal were the songs whereby a bridge of communion was builded during this period of preparation. Nearly all primitive peoples have invested prospective mothers with an aura of sanctity, asserting that throughout the nine months of pregnancy they are surrounded by Angels. Among highly organized Indian tribes, the homage paid to women during this period was most pronounced.

Orthodox Christianity is not very popular with the Navajo tribe because it sponsors a masculine Deity only and its culture is centered largely in the male aspect of Divinity. The principal Navajo Deity is feminine. Many of their most elaborate ceremonials give recognition to the fact that woman is supreme in the hogan and that children belong to the clan of the mother. In their enlightened symbology, the East belongs to the Earth Woman; the South to the Mountain Woman; the West to the Water Woman; the North to the Corn Woman. The importance of woman among the Iroquois is evidenced by the fact that to them is delegated the responsibility of choosing a chief; and there have been times when a woman served in that capacity.

MUSIC IN RELATION TO CHILD CULTURE

During the birth procedure the attending medicine man sang to the accompaniment of waving eagle feathers. With its head turned toward the sacred fire in the east, a newborn babe was bathed in cold water to make it brave. Its first feeding, looked upon as holy, consisted of pollen, a ceremonial food. And the infant's first laugh was a signal for the joyous rite of bestowing gifts. Naming of the child was a beautiful ceremony carried out to music replete with mysticism. Because it was believed to provide the little one with the protective power of an Angel Spirit, the name was most carefully chosen — unless, as frequently happened, it had been revealed to the mother-to-be in a dream or vision while she was in retirement for meditation. The Navajos gave every child a secret name never to be used except in cases of emergency. Later, if heavy winds were damaging a crop, that secret name was used in invocations to the Wind Spirit to cease its destructive rhythms.

Indians are great lovers of games. Every game taught to their children is for the purpose of developing some quality of mind or strengthening some attribute of character. To this day, their children's games, designed to fit them for assuming the obligations of adult life, are carefully chosen and supervised. Most of them center in the relationship between mother and child for she is their principal guardian.

Music and its appreciation provide the background for an Indian child's up-bringing, but not indiscriminate music such as our children are permitted to hear. Parents little realize the irritation that the discordant jazz rhythms of the average musical offering sets up in the delicate constitution of a child — irritation which tends toward outbursts of temper and serious ills of both mind and body. In his leaning toward the primitive, wiser is the American Indian than most moderns with all their vaunted superiority of education and culture.

True to traditions received by members of ancient tribes from their Masters of Wisdom, Indian music remains a sacred art, and is used as such. However, some of our red men, by reason of close proximity with their white brothers, have adopted modern ways and customs extending even into their musical field. In days of old the custom prevailed among various tribes of never permitting anyone of evil temper or oppressed with sorrow to enter the presence of a child lest discordant emanations lead to its illness or early death. From the very hour of conception, the incoming ego was surrounded with music — which prompts another reference to the magnificent physique and stately bearing of the purebred American Indian.

Indian lullabies are common among all tribes. There once existed an honorable profession followed by aged squaws of sitting beside a baby's cradle and singing to it for a number of hours each day. Lullabies have been the prized prerogative of mothers since time immemorial, and to Indian mothers were bequeathed lovely cradle songs. One of them, resonant with mysticism, intones the promise: "Sleep! Sleep! It will carry you into a land of wonderful dreams, and in these dreams you will see a future day."

As children grew up they were taught their own melodies. These were usually about birds and animals of the surrounding forests and plains with which they were familiar. The music was characteristic of the animals described. These musical stories were at a fast tempo when they were about a cat, a dog or a fox; when descriptive of a bear or cow the music was slow and ponderous. The little ones were thus taught to associate musical rhythms with the intimate details of their everyday life and to make them a part of their daily routine. Indians, wise in the lore of the soul, well knew that peace, beauty and harmony were the rightful heritage of every child.

INDIAN MUSICAL THERAPY AND BELIEF IN THE SUPERNATURAL

Frances Densmore, one of the best-known authorities on Indian lore, writes that "the early purpose of Indian music has frequently been designated as calling upon earth spirits for help or for summoning supernatural aid."

Among early Indians the thought was prevalent that music was essential to the demonstration of supernatural powers. Music, therefore, became an important part of the equipment of the medicine man who occupied the honored role of priest and physician to his tribe. The medicine man had to prove that he possessed the powers of the magician or wonder-worker before he was thought to be qualified for the office of healer. Since the Indians believed that healing was done by the intercession of discarnate and celestial spirits the healer necessarily had to be able to contact these other-world beings. Music was used as the bridge between the planes. Thus we see why the Indian concept of music was religious in nature, and music looked upon as a sacred art. His tastes did not incline toward secular music, although Indian music expressed all types of feeling and emotion, and included narrative songs and war chants. Nevertheless the essential nature of music was sacred, and even in modern times secular music is looked upon with disfavor. Music was dedicated to the spiritual needs of the individual, and to healing; not to passion and glorification of the person.

Through his close attunement with nature the Indian is a born clairvoyant, second sight coming to him naturally. In the medicine man this native facility was enhanced by means of a rigidly disciplined life including protracted periods of fasting and meditative prayer.

Numerous allusions to healing rituals occur in the tribal songs; and from these it would seem that the medicine men were aware of an inner plane assemblage which was a common source of power for healers of all tribes. This mysterious inner-plane Central Guild was symbolized by a white shell, and frequent references are made to the wonder-working powers of this talisman.

Faith is fundamental to all healing processes. Indian healing rituals show this very clearly. Songs used in treatment of illness were usually divided into two parts, one descriptive of the mystic powers of the healer and the other an affirmation of certainty that the patient would be restored to health. This is instanced in the words of an old Chippewa healing song: "You will recover, you will walk again. It is I who say it and my power is great. through our White Shell I will enable you to walk again."

The words of such songs were repeated several times, forcefully and with great solemnity, as the medicine man applied herbal lotions to wounds or bruises, or used the magnetic emanations of his hands. He was often assisted by his wife, both of them singing to the accompaniment of drum and rattle.

In the rhythms of their music lay its efficacy. The power intonations and rhythmic measures varied in the treatment of different diseases. Here is a fertile field of investigation for the music therapist! As Indian civilization retreats before the civilization of the white man, much of the ancient lore is lost and forgotten. Many of the healing chants are even now almost beyond understanding. Their deep occult significance has been lost. Frances Densmore expresses it well when she says that "the old Indian, taking his music with him, is passing quietly into the Great Silence."

Older members of various tribes comprehend something of the vast occult powers which attend upon the right use of their songs, and these are reverently passed on from one generation to the next. There is a saying among them that the old songs were "received in dreams" but that the new songs are *composed*. It is deplorable that practically no music is now being "received in dreams" in the ancient manner; and the reason is that few modern young people are willing to live the disciplined, renunciatory life necessary for such inner-plane communication.

The healing songs were all thought to be of supernatural origin, many coming to the medicine men in visions or dreams.

The neophyte who came to the Grand Healing Guild seeking to become a priest was put through various testings, and only after having passed through several initiatory degrees, reminiscent of the Mystery Temple work of ancient civilizations, could he be admitted to the Guild. All of the tribes drew knowledge from this Guild, but the techniques in each tribe tended to be the secret of the tribe, and were conveyed in drawings and signs that could be deciphered only by members of that one tribe. Each tribe received its own sacred teachings and these were kept inviolate for the benefit and enlightenment of the tribe.

As previously noted, healing songs were sung or intoned to the accompaniment of a drum or rattle; sometimes both were employed, and in the treatment of certain maladies the notes of a flute were used. The drum possessed a deep spiritual significance. Its decorations were symbolic, often representing the means by which a medicine man made contact or communicated with his discarnate teacher and the degree of Initiation he had attained. A rattle was also a sacred instrument, used only in religious ceremonials and in treating the sick.

It is a fact well worthy of notice that the Indian method of musical therapy emphasized the use of percussion instruments almost exclusively. On the contrary, modern techniques ban their use from a treatment room. In ancient times stringed instruments were practically unknown to the Indians while today strings have been proven the most effective in treating disease, as many hospital workers will testify. We must turn to the occultists for a satisfactory explanation of this contradictory procedure.

Man is much more than he appears to be to our limited physical vision. He possesses a series of tenuous, highly etherealized bodies which interpenetrate his dense physical form. With each succeeding generation these finer vehicles become increasingly sensitized. It is only the most insensate, the most materialistic person whose nerves can withstand the shock of a prolonged impact from percussion instruments exclusively. The over-placidity of the early Indian temperament needed acceleration while the over-emotional nature of modern man requires a soothing and quieting influence. Truly, in the words of the poet, "Music hath charms . . ." There is a musical antidote for every type of human ill. Percussion instruments awaken and stimulate. Strings make for calm and relaxation. The magic of healing with music is universal and its blessings belong to the Ages.

The supernatural forms in a large part the concepts upon which Indian civilization and culture rest. Specific beliefs vary with different tribes although fundamentals are similar. In accordance with Navajo concepts, incarnate and discarnate are so closely allied that they are grouped as one class, designated as "Earth Surface People." The Holy People are of a higher order, namely, Masters or Elder Brothers. Indians ascribe to them many powers and faculties not belonging to our ordinary world. They are believed to control the elements, walk on the rainbow, and perform many other supernatural feats.

Extended vision and superphysical faculties being common among Indians, their close affiliation with disembodied entities is almost universally recognized. The general belief among all tribes is that relatives and friends, with but slight change in appearance or manner, await the demise of the living, ready to accompany the newly dead through their period of adjustment on the other side of life.

The highest and most favored Deity among the Navajos is "Changing Woman," always young and beautiful. She dwells amid the western waters. "Blessing Way," the most important ceremonial of these people, is a ritual descriptive of how she teaches the most advanced Earth People to control fire, air, water and earth, and to harmonize all nature's forces. "Blessing Way" is but another name for Initiation. Through its power the celebrants come into intimate relationship with Changing Woman, the wife of the Sun, and are able to contact at will other members of the Holy People.

A prominent feature of the ceremonial of "Blessing Way" is the elevated likeness of Changing Woman, called a "dry painting." This likeness is made of crushed flower petals and the pollen of corn; it must be made only at specified holy seasons in especially consecrated areas, the work being done to the accompaniment of music by a definitely consecrated musician. In all such likenesses it is obligatory that four colors — white, blue, yellow and black — be used. These dry paintings of their great feminine Deity are conspicuous to this day in every hogan where the Rites of Blessing Way are observed. In all well-regulated families this ritual takes place at least every six months, and oftener if there is crisis or emergency.

The sacred likenesses are combined with "Curing Chants" of the medicine man in his treatment of all manner of disease. The regimen for both practitioner and patient is very strict, demanding sexual continence, a serious and thoughtful demeanor, and much time devoted to meditation and prayer.

Most significant among all tribes is the Puberty Initiation bestowed upon boys and girls aged seven to thirteen. Two neophytes or students of the medicine man are masked, one in white and one in black. The children are arranged in new-moon formation about a sacred fire, boys to the north, girls to the south. They are then escorted, one by one, to face the gods (masked men). The white-masked one marks the shoulders of each child with sacred cornmeal to the accompaniment of a weird, plaintive song by the black-masked one. The latter strikes the meal marks on the boys' bodies with some reeds bound together, completely changing the tones and rhythm of his song as he does this. In the case of girls, reeds are substituted by ears of corn carried in each hand and pressed against cornmeal marks. Black-mask places his mask over the face of each child in turn, and directs him or her to always look upward for continuous contact with the Holy People — this being the purpose of all Initiations, both ancient and modern. The reed used to touch certain spiritual centers to be awakened within the initiate-to-be represents the magic staff or wand within the spinal canal; the ear of corn symbolizes sacred androgynous power ascribed in certain mystery teachings to the Divine Feminine.

The manner and customs of varying civilizations change with the passing centuries, but symbolic ceremonies remain largely the same. Two principal schools of ceremonialism in the modern world retain much of ancient ritual. The four holy colors of the dry painting, the sacred fire, the traveling toward the East are all suggestive of Masonry. Homage to the Sacred Woman and Blessing Way are reminiscent of the Church's adoration of the Lady and the

,rotective use of the rosary. Certain it is that although it has many facets, Truth is one.

Among early Sioux tribes the puberty observance was most impressive. At the age of twelve or thirteen, and after a long and arduous preparation under the guidance of his parents, a boy underwent a severe and prolonged fast. During this time the youth sang over and over again his own particular "Vision Song" as he waited patiently for a vision of the spirit Helper who would be his teacher throughout his life. After Initiation, when he wished to call upon this teacher, it was only necessary to sing his Vision Song to become conscious of that presence.

During the vigil, the face of the boy was blackened with charcoal to betoken humility and dedication to selfless service. His future destiny was revealed to him in his vision. He saw himself as a medicine man, warrior or some other worthy member of the tribe, and returned home ready to begin training in accordance with his revelation. The strength and nobility portrayed by the vision accorded to the youth were supposed to be incorporated in his character by means of his own individual song. This, therefore, became an adult Indian's most precious gift, one he cherished throughout his whole life.

If no vision were granted, the youth was expected to endure another period of rigorous preparation and then make a second attempt to contact his spirit teacher. This failing, his father presented to him a dish containing charcoal with which to blacken his face and a second dish containing food symbolizing worldly ease. If he chose the latter he became practically an outcast from the tribe, for a man without a vision or a spiritual Helper was considered a failure, both physically and mentally.

Frances Densmore gives an interesting description of an old Indian custom prevailing among the Chippewas. Suspended on a pole in front of several Indian dwellings was an oblong white cloth whereon were depicted in colored paints various birds and animals. These pictures were symbols of dreams or Vision Songs which had never yet been sung because the magic power of the songs remained latent within the neophytes who had not brought them into manifestation.

The medicine man together with his healing music and various procedures constitute a fascinating study for students of occultism. As already said, music for healing is always of a slow tempo and steady rhythm strangely hypnotic in effect. While listening to it, an intuitive person is definitely conscious of its supernatural power. The words of these strange songs are repeated over and over. One of them intones: "Working at night I raise the person who is very sick. I have medicine power." When death is approaching he makes use of the weirdest of rhythms in an attempt to hold the spirit in its body as long as possible.

A medicine man must summon his invisible Helpers in a certain prescribed way else they will refuse to come to his assistance. He permits himself to be securely manacled, both hands and feet, and then placed in his teepee, usually before a sacred fire. He then sings and chants his own individual medicine songs far into the night. If Helpers incline to answer his petitions favorably, a rush of wind will sway the teepee violently and voices may be heard admonishing the healer and advising him how to proceed in his work of restoration. Freed of his manacles, he will come forth to indicate that powers have been vested in him for ministering to others.

INDIAN CEREMONIALISM

In dealing with the importance of ceremonialism in Indian life we naturally turn to the Pawnees, perhaps the supreme Indian mystics. Their religion consists chiefly of prophecy and vision, which are elaborated by impressive and ofttimes intricate rituals. Their religious observances center largely in a commemoration of the four Sacred Seasons: the Spring and Autumn Equinoxes, the Winter and Summer Solstices. The general pattern of Arapahoe worship also seems to be attuned to the number four. It is their tribal belief that by means of these four seasonal observances contact is established for the bestowal of supernatural powers and that these, in turn, will bring them health, wealth and long life.

There were four tribes among the Pawnees. Each tribe had its own chief and four principal officials, the Nahikuts, who worked directly under the supervision of their chief. Next in prominence to the chief were the priests who presided over the ceremonies. Third in rank were the medicine men and warriors. Fourth were the lay members of the tribes. There are still many secret societies among these tribes, each existing for the purpose of teaching various manifestations of supernatural power. The secret societies of all the tribes unite for the grand seasonal ceremonials.

Morning Star is the name of the principal masculine Deity; *Evening Star* is their principal goddess. These two preside over the four points of the heavens and the four Sacred Seasons, and mankind is their offspring. In addition they have four lodges of lesser gods who are the guardians of the medicine men, the warriors, various classes of leaders and the people.

The Pawnee ceremonial year begins with the spring observance, when the sacred seed corn is distributed with elaborate rites. Every lodge or teepee has its own altar containing sacred relics, one of the most cherished being the seed corn. On the altar is placed a bundle containing two ears of this corn, one dedicated to their masculine deity and one to their feminine. This spring festival is designated as the *Morning Star Ceremony*. Preparation for it is made with the utmost care, revealing the Pawnees to be true devotees of ceremonialism.

Morning Star rules the eastern heavens. Accompanied by the Sun and all the stars of the eastern heavens, he goes to woo Evening Star in the west. She sends her companion, the Moon, and her attendant stars of the western skies to meet them. Such is the symbolism of the ritual celebrating the Spring Equinox. The journey of Morning Star is fraught with ten grave perils, five being concerned with the difficulties of travel and five with attacks by wild animals. He conquers each peril by means of music. The final test is to overcome the huge serpent that bars his way. This he tames by means of song.

Strange as it may seem, this ceremonial depicts the

Path of Initiation into the Mysteries. We have many times stated that music as an aid in developing spiritual powers is an almost unexplored field. It is significant of the vast wealth of Indian mysticism to note that their use of music for this purpose antedates so-called civilized history. The Morning Star ceremonial continues for four days and four nights, the interval of the Equinox, and at times an invisible chorus can be heard joining in the songs.

The Harvest Ceremonial of the Autumn Equinox is celebrated with vigils, rites and sacrifices. The ritual is divided into two parts, a public observance for the tribesmen and a secret observance for an advanced few. This is the way the Mysteries have always been commemorated. The sacred bundles previously referred to are an important factor in this ritual. Designated as "Making Mother Corn," the two ears are placed in the sacred bundle of each family as a good-luck token for the following year.

The music and dancing accompanying the harvest observance are beautifully symbolic, often prophetic of safety or danger, and some of them are for the purpose of dispelling the fear of death. Friends or relatives frequently appear before the worshipers during these performances, the discarnates taking up the music by intoning words such as "I have returned — now you see me" or "Remember, when we pass from the old earth we pass to a new, where we are now." Another declares: "Yonder from whence I come, our relatives are walking." In the light of such musical intonements, it is not difficult to realize that communion between the living and the dead is very intimate.

The famous Sun Dance of the Pawnees commemorates the Summer and Winter Solstices. It is an expression of obedience to the spiritual impulses released at these seasonal high points. In certain parts of this dance the participants form a circle moving from east to west in harmony with the movement of the Sun. In another portion of the ritual the women do a series of six dances and the men a series of six, thus commemorating the work of the six masculine and the six feminine signs of the zodiac.

It is natural that the Indian, by reason of his great

love for and intimate, continuous contact with nature, finds it easy to attune his highest and most revered religious celebrations to nature's cosmic rhythms. His oneness with the beauty and harmony of nature is expressed with rare delicacy of feeling in the song: "As my eyes search the vastness of the prairie, I can feel the summer in the spring."

Only certain Initiates are eligible to go into the forest to search for the Sun Dance pole. Their every move, from dedication to the quest until they return with the sacred tree, is deeply and beautifully symbolic. The place of the ceremonial is circular in form, representative of the heavens, and in this enclosure the consecrated pole is set up. That part of the ceremonial which is public begins with an imposing processional led by the priests, who chant a beautiful poetical ritual pregnant with a meaningful interpretation of the ceremonial. The priests are followed by dances in appropriate costume. Their motions are graceful, stately, and dignified, and in complete harmony with the solemnity and impressiveness of the occasion. The dancers always gaze unflinchingly into the heart of the sun, and by their poses symbolize a divine at-one-ment with that bright Presence. The secret rites of the Solstices portray the process of bringing about the splendors of a new life.

These seasonal observances constitute the most important phase of tribal life, and the conclusion of one is the signal for beginning preparation for the next.

Even this brief survey shows what a glorious occult background lies behind Indian civilization. Their religion, their art, their way of life are but outer reflections of this rich heritage of spiritual truths.

Chapter VI

RECENT DEVELOPMENTS IN MUSIC THERAPY

MUSIC AS MEDICINE

IT IS CLEARLY EVIDENT that the New Age is producing a new science of healing; leastwise, we may say it is new. Although its basic elements are more ancient than Pythagoras, our age is rediscovering them in a manner uniquely its own. This new version is, and yet is not, the musical science of the Mysteries. Evolution recapitulates spirally; and, on each ascending arc of the spiral, ancient knowledge reappears in a more advanced form.

The famous Greek physician Hippocrates administered musical treatments to his patients as early as 400 B.C.; yet this type of treatment did not originate with him, but merely found in him an exponent of the first order. With the increasing materialism of Western civilization, the major tenets of ancient musical therapy have been either forgotten or deliberately discarded.

Wars have been described as "operations for spiritual cataract." In spite of their horror and ugliness — or rather, because of them — man turns within for consolation and strength. He seeks solace in things beautiful and true for they are of the soul. Thus, during the course of the last war music was drawn upon more and more for healing ministrations by both orthodox and unorthodox practitioners.

Members of the medical fraternity are beginning to recognize musical therapy as a scientific branch of healing practice. Some have even admitted that musical therapy may have great possibilities. This points to notable advances in New Age techniques which no doubt have been accelerated by the world's urgent need for augmented remedial measures.

Speaking before a convention of the Music Teachers National Association, Dr. Ira Altschuler, of the Eloise State Hospital of Michigan, stated that eventually a musical therapist will compound prescriptions after the manner of a pharmacist, and that all musical prescriptions should be written by persons having a clear knowledge and understanding of man's mental and emotional mechanism. He further declared that he considered neurosis to have been the great scourge of World War II, claiming two-thirds of the army discharges were due to his malady.

In an article titled *Music Is Medicine,* Doren Antrim writes: "It has been found that musical vibrations make their impact upon the entire body, being picked up by the nerves, spinal column and even by the bones. This is why persons who are deaf can react to music. It has also been demonstrated," he continues, "that music affects the pulse, respiration and blood pressure; but its deepest effects, and those from which most of its curative properties are derived, are mental and emotional. And since each person's emotional setup is different, music therapy must necessarily be a matter of individual prescription."

Apropos of the foregoing, this excerpt is from an article that appeared in the press some time ago: "How would you like to fill the doctor's prescription at the music store rather than the drug store . . . a symphony or sonata for that sinus, some Debussy for the feeling of debility, Bach for the ache in your back, and Mozart for mumps and measles? It has always been supposed that music could mix with medicine, but only recently has any organized attempt been made on a large scale to determine just what the proper dose should be."

SONG OF PLANETARY RHYTHMS

"The Word was with God, and the Word was God." Thus the inspired Apostle John intoned his immortal *Song of Planetary Rhythms.* From the most minute atom to the greatest star, every manifestation is an echo of that creative Word, and each cell of man's organism vibrates to the rhythm of this universal song. It is the fundamental law of health, and by it was man made "in the image and likeness of God." Had he continued to live in harmony with it, disease and bodily malformations would have been unknown to him.

In the etheric body are centered the forces animating man's physical vehicle, so disease is evidenced in the etheric before it manifests in the physical. The etheric, composed of finer, more attenuated substances than the physical, is correspondingly more amenable to vibratory influences. It is upon the former that harmony and rhythm have the most potent effect. Good music readjusts its molecular structure in accordance with the original divine plan, the archetype, and refines and accentuates its vibratory currents. All forms of beauty and harmony increase this regenerating process.

ORIGIN AND EXPANSION OF MUSICAL THERAPY

The strong modern trend toward musical treatment of many forms of illness, nervous and mental ailments especially, is really not new. It has a precedent of many centuries. For example, Egyptian documents unearthed at Kahum mention the use of musical treatments back in 2500 B.C. Thales, six centuries before Christ, tells of curing the plague with song. Philip V of Spain found that four songs sung to him every evening alleviated his mental apathy. New Age development is recapturing long-forgotten sciences, musical therapy among them. In 400 B.C. Hippocrates, the "father of medicine," took his mental patients to listen to music in the Temple of Esculapius, the God of Healing. Homer wrote that music caused a cessation of Ulysses' hemorrhage. Flute playing was recommended by early Greeks as a remedy for sciatica.

During her Golden Age, Greece was the home of art and beauty. Much of her wisdom lore will be brought to light in the Aquarian Age, when there will be a rebirth of art and beauty on an even higher level. Once again the ways of the artist and healer are merging. To be beautiful is to be well, and to be well is to come into attunement with nature. As Keats, an inspired poet, sings.

Beauty is truth, truth beauty — that is all
Ye know on earth, and all ye need to know.

AN EXPERIMENT IN MUSICAL THERAPY

The following excerpt was published in the *London
Daily Times* and is a most interesting demonstration of the
power and magic of music. It is a description of work
done by the Wingfield Music Club of Great Britain and
Northern Ireland. To quote:

> This unusual club is an attempt to use practical musicianship
> as therapy for cripples, spastics, asthmatics, "blue babies," and
> other disabled people, mostly children. An equally important part
> of its function is to give these handicapped players a sense of
> achievement, the creative comradeship of ensemble playing, and a
> niche in the community.

HOW IT BEGAN

The idea originated some years ago when Mr. Herbert Lyon, a
keen amateur violinist, injured three fingers of his left hand, involv-
ing a spell in hospital, contact with other disabled folk, and a
hard struggle to master his disability and play again. It occurred
to him that what he could achieve others might also, given a big
enough incentive, and that music might provide, indeed, that
incentive.

Beginning with a six-year-old daughter of a neighbor, Herbert
Lyon set about testing his theories. The first problem was to find
the most suitable instrument for the child, who had an artificial left
hand. After various experiments, Mrs. Lyon's cello, played "in
reverse" with the higher strings nearest the bowing arm, was found
to be the best; the bow was kept in place in the artificial hand with
strong elastic.

It was nine months before the little girl could play the first
bars of "Ba Ba Black-sheep"; but 18 months after that she played
a solo, and in a trio at the local youth music festival. After this
achievement the education authorities, convinced the girl would
benefit from professional teaching, provided a suitable instrument
and granted tuition fees.

Meanwhile, Mr. Lyon's interest in teaching handicapped children had developed. His wife became interested too, and so did
friends. "Sunday mornings at our house were chaotic. In the front
room someone would be having a piano lesson, violins were scraping
away in the dining room; upstairs, recorders and dulcimers were
in the bedrooms. Even my small office and at one time even the
bathroom was occupied by somebody hard at practice." Eventually
the offer of a school hall and some practice rooms once a week
solved the accommodation problem, and the club as it is today
came into being.

VOLUNTARY HELP

Membership fluctuates around 60 — several members may be in hospital at any given moment, and a score or so of volunteers; housewives, businessmen, school teachers — help with the organization, and transport arrangements, as well as with the individual lessons. "The enthusiastic amateur makes the best teacher at first," says Mr. Lyon. Later, promising children can be passed on to professional teachers, fees being paid by the club or the local authority. Instruments, even costly ones, seem to turn up almost miraculously as needed, often as gifts. Musical instrument firms have been interested and helpful, and leading professional musicians have given generously of help, advice, and interest.

One principle of Mr. Lyon's work is never to give any child an instrument that is within his or her compass. He prefers to present a challenge. Thus, when a girl with chronic bronchitis was brought to him, he decided she should learn the oboe, as an incentive to master her breathing problems; the girl recently won a junior exhibition at Trinity College of Music, one of five club members to do so, and her bronchitis is a thing of the past.

A boy who could not stand unaided was taught the violin and then encouraged not merely to stand to play a concert solo but actually to walk on to the platform. A spastic with little co-ordination may be put on to percussion instruments, calling in rhythm in the service of control. In this way the children learn much more than the actual music. Shown that their fingers can be trained, some have gone on to master typing and other skills, and have become capable of earning a living.

REAL SUCCESS

Perhaps the club's most remarkable achievement so far has been with Janet Cattier, a severe spastic, unable to speak and almost completely lacking in control of her hands. She learned the recorder first. "It was amazing to watch her, her right hand curled completely underneath it; but this girl really was a trier, and after making some progress, she came to me and, in her own way, indicated that she wished to learn the violin. Those first days had to be seen to be believed. More often than not, the violin finished on the floor; the bow pointing anywhere, giving the impression sometimes that she was fencing rather than fiddling." Yet when the club gave its first public concert the child had improved enough to play a violin duet with Bert Lyon. About this time the girl also began to attempt to compose music and was eventually placed with a teacher of composition. Now she has added the piano to her studies, has mastered speech control, and has recently begun work as a clerk — *without* having to be registered as a disabled person.

MUSICAL THERAPY AND THE STARS

Probably the most interesting of experimentations in connection with healing by music are those dealing with

[104]

cases of psycho-neurosis. Among pioneers in this field was Harriet Ayers Seymour of New York City. That such leaders will be divinely inspired, and their work brought to public recognition at the phychological moment, has long been the teaching of spiritual science. This was true in the case of Mrs. Seymour. After many years of research, in 1941 she organized the National Foundation of Musical Therapy in New York. Since then several hundred musicians have been trained to meet the urgent need presented by a "neurosis epidemic." Furthermore, musical therapy has been introduced into the army medical center at the Walter Reed Hospital in Washington, D.C. Under orders from the Surgeon General, the results of this modern method of treating human ills will be carefully charted by army doctors.

People of the United States are strongly Geministic in temperament and Gemini characteristics are restlessness, eagerness and alertness. Its natives want to be on the move in quest of the new, the untried, the unusual. "Nerves" are their principal affliction. To wit, the above physician's statement that two-thirds of the United States discharges for illness were for some form of neurosis. It would be interesting to compare this percentage with that of other nations at war. Undoubtedly, America would be well in the lead.

A spiritual scientist who traces causes to their starry origin approaches the study of musical therapy from a different viewpoint than that taken by the majority of modern investigators. To him astrological correlations are important. For example, the keynote of Gemini is F Sharp. Compositions written in this key have a direct action upon man's nervous system, which comes under Gemini's rulership.

As has been noted, musical prescriptions should resemble those of a pharmacist and would prove more remedial if the stellar ingredient were properly taken into account. For the best results, the type of instrument and the music must vary in accordance with the nerve complication under consideration. To produce relaxation of nerves that refuse to let go because of excessive strain, a harp is recommended as the best instrument and compositions in F Sharp, with minor notes played almost as an undertone. If the patient can be in a room decorated in pastel shades of spring green or mauve, and the environment be one of peace and freedom from any sudden or startling noise, such music should produce complete release from nerve tension followed by a long period of restful, restorative sleep.

Another quieting keynote is A Major (three sharps), the key of Aquarius and of man's etheric body wherein are centered the nerve currents (vital forces) of his physical body. Nerve exhaustion responds to this Aquarian key, especially when played on a piano or violin in a room done in daffodil yellow. Excessive mental derangement responds to the keys of F Sharp and A Major varied at intervals by F Major (one flat), the keynote of Sagittarius, ruler of the higher mind. Patients so suffering need the most soothing of string instruments, preferably a harp, and treatment rooms should be in restful tints of green.

Spiritual scientists recognize that the complex organism known as man's body has been built according to vibratory sound patterns, and that it is sustained by the keynotes emitted by the twelve creative Hierarchies. Each of these Hierarchies sets its impress on a particular portion of the body.

D Flat Major is the musical keynote of Aries which rules the head and its many varied functions. Its familiar diseases are cerebral hemorrhage and glaucoma.

E Flat Major is the keynote of Taurus, which governs the throat, neck and ears. Familiar diseases under Taurus are tonsilitis and mastoiditis.

F Sharp, as has been noted, is the keynote of Gemini. It rules the lungs, shoulders, arms and hands. Its most familiar diseases are tuberculosis and arthritis.

G Sharp Major is the keynote of Cancer, which rules the stomach and its functions; also the solar plexus. Stomach ulcers and gallstones are its principal diseases.

A Sharp Major is Leo's keynote, the sign that rules the heart and the spinal cord. Heart disease in many forms comes under Leo.

C Natural Major is the musical keynote of Virgo, the sign that rules the large and small intestines. Its most common malady is appendicitis.

D Major is the keynote of Libra, ruler of the kidneys and adrenal glands. Bright's disease is its affliction.

E Major is the keynote of Scorpio, governor of the organs of procreation. Infection of the prostate gland is active in males.

F Major is the keynote of Sagittarius, which governs the hips, thighs and the sacral plexus at the base of the spine. Sciatica is the predominating disease under this sign.

G Major is the keynote of Capricorn, ruler of the knees. As a reflex action from Cancer (its opposite sign) various stomach disabilities may show up through swollen knees.

A Major keynotes Aquarius, which governs the lower limbs and ankles. Rheumatism predominates as its malady.

B Major is the spiritual keynote of Pisces, the sign that rules the feet. Its foremost disability is malformation of the feet and toes.

Every sign receives an impress from its opposite sign. Hence, in females severe throat afflictions in childhood will often be followed after puberty by irregular menses together with ovarian and uterine complications.

Each of the seven planets is correlated to two signs. The Sun and Moon relate to one sign each, Leo and Cancer respectively. The planetary relationships are as follows:

MERCURY — Gemini and Virgo
VENUS — Taurus and Libra
MARS — Aries and Scorpio
JUPITER — Sagittarius and Pisces
SATURN — Capricorn and Aquarius
NEPTUNE — Pisces

The four predominating systems of the body are each ruled by one major planet, in the astrological sense, and other planets govern subsidiary effects. The muscular system is ruled by Mars, planet of action; the nervous systems by Mercury, with Mars having a lesser rulership of motor nerves and the Moon of the sympathetic system. The brain generally is ruled by Mercury, which also has chief governance of the right hemisphere, with Mars ruling the left. Heart and spleen are ruled by the Sun, the bony structure by Saturn. The glandular system as a whole is ruled by Uranus, with each gland individually also showing response to other planetary rulers. The pituitary gland is under the rulership of the planet Uranus and the sign Aquarius. The pineal gland is under the rulership of the planet Neptune and the sign Pisces. These two glands are located in the head.

Thus we may note that the human body truly bears the imprint of divinity, the impress of the twelve zodiacal Hierarchies, from head to toe. The purpose of man's earthly pilgrimage is to perfect his body that it may be a fitting temple for the indwelling spirit.

This is but a brief outline of the effects planets have on certain parts of the body, together with their zodiacal and planetary correlations. When there is an affliction, planetary keynotes can be calculated, and therapeutic music prescribed. It is only a matter of time until an accurate diagnosis will be made by means of the keynotes of the heavenly orbs as shown by a natal horoscope and as indicated by planetary progressions and transits.

Chapter VII

RECENT DEVELOPMENTS IN MUSIC
THERAPY—continued

ADVERSE EFFECTS OF JAZZ

UNDER NO CONDITION whatever should swing rhythms, popularly termed *jazz,* be permitted in a sick room. As already observed, jazz had its origin in the infant period of the human race, when it was used for the purpose of stimulating an almost static desire (astral) body in its first stage of development. The irregular currents of this so-called music acted almost directly upon the desire nature, producing excitability, accelerating heart and blood beat, arousing emotions — thus bringing about a result opposite to what "musical medicine" is designed to achieve.

One authority states that jazz has no place in a hospital because its irregular beat and lack of form are definitely disturbing and so delay healing. In previous writings dealing with music as a healing and regenerative treatment, we have referred to the serious consequences suffered by adolescents who listen regularly and indiscriminately to this type of rhythm. *Eliminate jazz and watch delinquency among youth decrease* is the substance of a statement by no less authority than the late Arthur Rodzinski, formerly a director of the New York Philharmonic Orchestra. "Jive type of music is a large contributing factor to a war degeneracy," he added, along with the comment that he saw no need for swing music so long as there were such beautiful compositions as the Strauss waltzes to provide dance tempo. Asked what he thought about jazz, Walter Damrosch, another great impressario, replied to the effect that music to be worthy of the name had to appeal either to the head or the heart; that jazz did neither. "It is a nerve irritant," he concluded.

RESPONSE OF THE INSANE TO MUSIC

Insanity is the result of a lack of co-ordination between the ego and its several invisible or finer bodies. Music therapy is highly effective in its action upon the emotions. Therefore, emotional conflicts — usually compounded of fear and frustrated desires — that are frequently the cause of insanity will yield to the curative powers of harmony where medical and physical therapy fail. This is due to the fact that musical harmonies restore the sundered link between the desire body and the ego, eliminating the conflict by establishing a condition of spiritual integrity, strength and stability.

There are numberless examples of the insane being healed by music. Many instances of such restoration are coming to the attention of the public, one of which is the case of a girl who performed over a San Francisco radio hook-up. "Miss Y appeared before a microphone at station KYA," stated a news report, "as a climax to music therapy treatments which have been employed in an effort to return her to normalcy. Another girl who is emotionally disturbed, identified only as Mrs. X, was to have appeared with Miss Y, but was unable to be present. So Miss Y, who is in her early twenties, played a difficult piano duet of Beethoven's original composition for four hands with Miss Margaret Tilly, concert pianist and expert in musical therapy." The report went on to say that Miss Y was no more than normally nervous as the hour of the broadcast approached, and did not suffer from "mike fright." Critics pronounced her skill as above average.

Miss Tilly explained that Miss Y's case was not the same as that of Mr. X who performed in Detroit under similar circumstances. She said that Mr. X had been an accomplished musician whereas Miss Y had not studied music extensively in the past. After only ten weeks of musical therapy Mr. X had recovered his sanity and was able to take up the study of music once more following a hiatus of nine years. Miss Y, whose condition was of about a year's duration, developed "an intense interest in musical performance while undergoing musical therapy treatments."

Experimentation with patients in the Chicago Hospital for the Insane revealed that awakening happy memories by playing old familiar melodies frequently restored a patient to rational thinking. A young mother, whose mind was so deranged at the time of childbirth that she hated her baby, was restored upon hearing a Brahm's lullaby her mother used to sing to her. An Italian girl, who had refused to speak to anyone for several months, broke her silence while listening to *O Sole Mio,* a famous Italian love ballad she had sung as a child.

According to the theory of Dr. Altschuler of Detroit, the influence of music is centered in the lower brain which is not affected by mental derangement. Spiritual scientists know this as the *feminine* brain center, seat of the subconscious mind. It is not only the storehouse of recollections from the current earth life, but is also a reservoir of memories carried over from previous incarnations — although these latter memories are not usually available to one's conscious mind until the cardiac and solar plexuses are awakened through spiritual work, a process wherein music is of inestimable value.

Insanity, Dr. Altschuler continues, is really the rebellion of a person against certain experiences over which he has no control. Becoming frustrated, the individual sets up a dream world and enters into it. The work of the healer, therefore, is to draw the patient out of his make-believe world and focus his interests upon normal activities of the objective realm.

According to this authority, the conscious mind centers in the cortes (upper brain) which esotericists call the masculine or positive brain. This is the area where mental disease becomes established. The seat of feelings and emotions is in the lower brain, the feminine or negative brain center. The latter, it appears, is not involved in mental maladies. Music, declares the doctor, affects and influences a patient through this lower brain center. Musical therapy meets no barrier of mental derangement as does either the written or spoken word that works through the upper or conscious area. This discovery, he concludes, makes music a unique and most potent remedial agency.

It is far more effectual for correcting disruption between man's several vehicles than is generally recognized. Under the focused power of the therapist's divine spirit within himself, wonderful healings have occurred, for harmony is the builder of the human body-temple just as inharmony is its destroyer.

Another instance of vital interest in this connection was related in a Detroit newspaper some years ago. An insane man, forty-five years of age, was an inmate of the Wayne County General Hospital psychiatric ward. His ailment was described by Dr. Altschuler as "a form of negativism resulting from a split personality." He had been under treatment in that institution for over eight years without any signs of improvement. Then it was decided to try music therapy, the man having once been a gifted pianist. At first this seemed to make little impression upon him, but before long he began to recover his former technical skill. Finally, it was arranged by the doctor for him to perform before a conference of the Music Teachers' National Association attended by three hundred musicians. They were enthralled by his masterly rendition of compositions by Chopin, Mozart and Beethoven and applauded thunderously, pronouncing the man to be a genius. His face an expressionless mask, he responded by a perfunctory bow and left the platform. Much had been gained yet something was still lacking. According to the article, the doctors were hoping that in time music would bring about the musician's complete recovery and thus demonstrate its value in treating the mentally ill.

Dr. Altschuler's attitude toward his mental cases approaches very close to the understanding of occult scientists. He arrived at his conclusion as the result of years of study and investigation of insanity. He states it must be understood that insane persons are not feeble-minded or basically different from normal persons. Their ailment is maladjustment to environment, and the cure is to be found in supervised therapy.

THE TECHNIQUE OF MUSIC-MEDICINE

Man is a composite being. He possesses vehicles finer than his physical body. In a normal person these vehicles are properly aligned and are under the control of the divine self. In an abnormal individual, especially one suffering from insanity, there is a break between the controlling ego and one or more of these subtle bodies. If the breach occurs between the emotional (desire) body and the ego, the insanity is of a type where the patient is given to cunning and to irresponsible actions. If the severed link is between the concrete mind and the ego, the patient is erratic and irrational. If the break is between the higher mind and the ego, he becomes a soulless creature capable of perpetrating inhuman and diabolical deeds.

The Veteran's Administration hospitals throughout the country have been using music therapy in many such cases with marked success. Patients are divided into two general groups: the non-responsive and the hyper-active. Professional musicians are called upon by attending physicians to arrange suitable programs for each group.

For instance, Kenneth Stanton, VA musical chief at the southeastern branch hospital, suggested the following program to stimulate non-responsive patients:

Prayer and Dream Pantomime from *Hansel and Gretel* by Humperdinck
Clair De Lune by Debussy
Dance of the Reed Flutes from Tschaikovsky's *Nutcracker Suite* then building up to
Sousa's *El Capitan March* or the finale to the
Fifth Symphony by Tschaikovsky

It is seen that music for the hard-to-arouse should begin softly and increase in tempo and volume. By the time the last stirring number has been played, most of the patients have been quickened to active interest.

Just the opposite is needed to quiet those who are under intense emotional strain. The music should start with violent chords and crescendos to attract their attention; then it should decrease to the soft tones of soothing compositions. For hyper-active patients, Stanton recommends selections from Borodin's *Prince Igor Overtures* as an opening, and *The Evening Star* from Wagner's *Tannhauser* or Bach-Gounod's *Ave Maria* to close. Complex harmonies should be avoided because they tend to cause confusion and worry. Where music is in a minor mode it has a depressing effect so should never be used.

Music-medicine treatment usually begins with a theme song, preferably some familiar childhood air. As an accompaniment, a violin, piano, cello and flute have proven to be a most effective combination. A pianist employed on the regular hospital staff has charge of the program arrangement.

MUSICAL THERAPY COMPLEMENTS SURGERY

In recent years the terrible results of the war have included a breaking down of both bodies and minds. Hence, curative needs have so multiplied as to turn the attention of psychiatrists, anaesthetists, and even orthodox medical practitioners toward any and every remedial possibility. A few outstanding individuals have instituted a foundation for the study of and experimentation with musical therapy, setting into motion projects that have proven beyond a doubt the great value of this form of treatment.

In Pennsylvania Dr. Van de Wall and in Massachusetts Dr. W. F. Searles have used it in their hospitals with marked success. And we have already mentioned that Mrs. Harriet Seymour, as a climax to her long, unstinted service via music in camp hospitals during World War II, established the New York Foundation of Musical Therapy. Dr. Van de Wall reported that the physiological and psychological benefits of music after surgery were especially noted in cases complicated by mental disorders. Also, as said before, Dr. Altschuler found rhythmic treatments of great benefit in hundreds of cases during the years following the war.

Music as an accompaniment to an anaesthesia is reported to be a regular practice in the operating rooms of the Chicago University medical clinics. It was first tested at the clinics in 1947 and was so successful in lessening the tension of patients undergoing major surgery that it was adopted as a standard procedure in connection with local, regional and spinal anaesthesia. The music is wired to the operating rooms from a central recorder room. Two channels of recordings are cut on a strip of magnetic tape that will play without interruption for four hours. Patients have a choice as to the music they prefer.

A Danish hospital has gone one step further. Surgery patients under local anaesthesia listen to music through head phones during their operation.

MUSIC AS A MORAL FORCE

. . . Their savage eyes turn'd to a modest gaze by the sweet power of music.
                                                                    —Shakespeare

Some criminals, probably most of them, have but little patience with sermonizing of any kind. Even the kindest and most reasonable words fail to touch them. But truly, there is none "So stockish hard and full of rage, but music for the time does change his nature." Hence it has been well said that "Where words end, there music begins."

Tonal harmony sets its impress upon deranged minds and broken bodies, and it is also a healing balm for broken hearts and shattered lives. It has saved many from prison who might otherwise be there, and it can do much to reclaim those who have already entered. It is illuminating to learn that out of sixty-one hundred and fourteen inmates in one British prison only six were musicians. A number of penal authorities, realizing the importance of music in relation to men's moral and physical well being, have introduced music into each day's activities. The inmates' day begins and ends with music. Harmonious and uplifting strains sound as an accompaniment to meals and recreation, because an atmosphere purified and lightened by the inspiration of good music is an antidote to a spirit of discontent or the machinations of those who are evil minded.

Music at the close of a prisoner's day is most important. The solitude of his cell during the night hours is often conducive to the resentment and sullen hatred which chalk out the pattern of future crimes if and when opportunity affords. Cheerful, stimulating evening concerts tend to dissipate pessimistic and sinister thoughts and replace them with optimistic and constructive ideas. They may even serve to lift the listeners into attunement with the Supreme Musician. On Enrico Caruso's visit to Atlanta, he of the magic voice, was asked by one of the inmates to sing for them. He did so. Shortly thereafter the following verses by a prisoner, appeared in the institution's paper:

We sit in our rows of sodden grey,
Up there in the great blank hall,
    Through the window bars the great blue day
And the golden sunshine call;
    Call us as Christ called Lazarus dead
To rise and come forth from his grave.
    Better the dead through the living dead
Whom the world shuts out and the bars shut in,
    Man-made scapegoats of all men's sins.
    Then in the hush of the great, blank hall
God wrought a wondrous miracle.
    For a voice like a glorious trumpet call
Arose as a soul from the depths of hell.
    And our souls rose with it on wondrous wings,
Rose from their prison of iron and clay,
    Forgot the grime and the shame of things,
Sin and grief and punishment—all—
    Were lost in that human trumpet call.
    Not bars nor banishment can abate
The strong, swift wings of the deathless soul
    Soaring aloft over grief and hate
As the tones of the music master roll
    Through the gloom and doom of flowering song
Into hearts that remember youth again.
    How then, if such be music's spell,
Shall we doubt that Christ still conquers hell?

IMPRESS OF COLOR AND MUSIC UPON CHILDREN

A well-known saying states "Give me a child until he is seven and you may have him the rest of his life." Doubtless the most important years in a child's life are those from one to seven. During this period he is highly impressionable, imaginative and imitative. Parents would be wise to guard carefully their words and actions in the presence o' children of such tender years, for they will naturally copy whatever they hear or see. Habits then formed are likely to stay with them throughout the rest of their lives. Thus parents are responsible for either great good or much harm to the character of their offspring.

During these years the vital body is in the process of formation — the body wherein impressions *set* their seal. Many elderly persons given to retrospection discover that dates, names and places associated with the first septenary of their lives have left a more lasting impression upon their memory than those of later years.

Colors should play an important role in the lives of every young person. Give children gayly colored toys. Surround them with various colors and note carefully those for which they evidence a preference. Oftentimes a baby in its second year will display a marked attraction to some colors and an aversion to others. You can learn much regarding a youngster's real nature by studying his reactions to music and color vibrations.

During a little one's first seven years the imagination has full play. Never try to stifle it. Instead, seek to develop it constructively for it is the image-building faculty of the soul. During that age children are still very near the fairy world so they revel in fairy tales. By relating colors to the stories it is easy to arouse interest in the power and magic of various hues without forcing on them colors for which they show an aversion. High-spirited, energetic children should be dressed in the duller, more subdued tones; those who tend to be shy and reticent will respond to richer, more vibrant colors; those who are highly sensitive or exceedingly nervous need the soft, pastel shades.

Also, let them listen to music that has a definite rhythm, but only that which is harmonious. Sousa's marches are splendid. As they listen, encourage them to express their feelings in pantomime or spontaneous dancing. It is well for them to give vent to such emotions as are aroused by whatever is noble and beautiful. There is available a great variety of records suitable to early childhood. A fine example is *Peter and the Wolf*. Teach children to distinguish between the different bird calls and intersperse the music with stories descriptive of the intelligence of birds and the loyalty of animals. Those who have this type of training early in life are not likely to use sling shots to murder feathered creatures or climb trees to rob nests when they are older.

During the years from seven to fourteen a child's color tastes become well formulated. Children in this age bracket should have their own rooms or, at least, some area they can call their own where they can surround themselves with colors to their liking. Furthermore, it is well not to compel them to learn to play a musical instrument for which they have no affinity. If at all possible, give them lessons on the instrument they like best, for every boy or girl should have some musical training. Wise is the parent who uses every means at his or her command to divert the interest of their children away from jazz, especially during the second septenary of their lives when their desire nature is in process of formation. Jazz has a tendency to quicken and intensify the desire nature. Hence, it is a grave mistake for young children to listen indiscriminately to so-called popular music — a common practice in altogether too many homes today.

A most delightful custom is to complete an evening study hour with a twenty- to thirty-minute concert. For this period choose music that is gay and melodious, such as Chaminade's *Scarf Dance, The Song of the Lark,* the *Berceuse* from *Jocelyn,* Victor Herbert's *Badinage;* and lovely numbers like *Traumerei, Humoresque,* Schubert's *Ave Maria,* Handel's *Largo;* yes, and von Weber's *Invitation to the Dance* and the *March of the Toy Soldiers* by Herbert. If a child appears tired or irritable conclude the music immediately lest you defeat the very purpose you are trying to accomplish. Programs should be carefully worked out that the children actually anticipate their musical hour as a period of relaxation and pleasure, a lovely interlude between the close of a busy day and the hours of sleep.

If children have received this type of musical training, by the time they reach fourteen they are ready to attend philharmonic concerts. As the result of such care and thought bestowed upon them during their formative years, they will have a rich heritage that will become ever more valuable as the years pass; that heritage is the ability to understand and appreciate good music when they hear it.

Chapter *VIII*

EXPERIMENTATION WITH MUSIC UPON THE PLANT KINGDOM

Thought Communication by Means of Music

Music is a form of expression from the first. On the first plane it heals, brings souls to attention, softens and causes the first heavy stillness to lift. For such uses, music is much needed. It is used by the workers and the people who have found their balance. On the second plane it is used a great deal, and from this plane onward becomes ever more beautiful. Music will appear to some as color, but music is a different vibration. Color can be instantly flashed to great distances. Music can go much further when it is associated with thought, for there is no limit to the carrying power of thought. By thought one can throw to an infinite distance a beautiful phrase or even a nocturne.

—From *Living Toward Mastership* by Beulah Armstrong

Laplanders' Recognition of the Power of Sound

*L*APLANDERS, WHO LIVE in the Arctic region of Scandinavia, possess remarkable knowledge about the therapeutic qualities of sound. They practice what is called lip reading, based on the belief that every condition of man's body and mind is related to certain sounds and words. Living as they do in a natural state, they retain much of primeval wisdom. Certain of their priests, like medicine men of American Indians and African aborigines, have a psychic sensitivity whereby they can determine the specific keynote of bodily organs and of ailments which require treatment. Thus informed, they intone the sounds and utter the words that will strengthen the organ and dispel the disease.

The factual basis for magical healing by means of invoking spiritual powers — ascribed by ancient Egyptians to a being known as the God of Words — is now verified by physical science, which has produced electronic instruments of such refinement that the vibratory frequency of every malady and of every organ of the body can be accurately tabulated and treated accordingly.

[119]

The Lapps believe that everything has a relationship to sound, a relationship that varies with age and changing conditions. So closely attuned are they to unspoiled nature that they even recognize the influence of the seasons of the year on the sound values of all natural phenomena. To Laplanders everything emits its individual keynote. These are looked upon as so many fragments which, when unified, compose the symphony of nature. These people are fully aware that in this fact is a deep spiritual significance, and they desire to so think and live as to bring their being into harmony with nature's rhythms.

In historical sequence, percussion instruments came first; then strings, and later wind instruments. The first provide rhythm; the second, harmony; the third, melody. This threefold function of music corresponds to the three-fold structure of man. Wind instruments are lifted to the musician's head and made audible by his breath. String instruments are related to his heart center; the violin, most sensitive and expressive of all musical instruments, rests on the musician's breast. Percussion instruments, related to man's limbs, are best represented by the drum because it is placed below the performer's hips and its rhythm incites the hearer to motion, especially to marching.

Melody and rhythm are the two components of ancient music. The third, harmony, was of later development. Harmony unfolds as the heart quality comes into expression. It is of the spirit and is central to man's very being. Like spirit, music is of the heaven world. It progressively permeates human organisms until they will be brought eventually into full harmony with the Music of the Spheres. It has the power to restore man to his all-but-forgotten divine estate. From this estate he came and to it he is destined to return. In our Western civilization music has been one of the principal factors in saving man's spirit from completely succumbing to the benumbing effects of materialism and mechanization.

How Plants Respond to Music

In connection with musical therapy, one of the most interesting fields of investigation is the effect of music on the plant kingdom. A pioneer in this field of exploration was the late famous Indian scientist, Sir Jagadas Chundar Bose, whose research is being continued at the Annamalai University of India. Scientists in a number of agricultural colleges in this country are working along similar lines. And with the growing awareness of hitherto undreamed-of forces in nature and their myriad applications — as, for example, in the field of electronics — there is not the readiness there once was to dismiss as non-existent influences that were long regarded as pure abstractions. The subjection of plants to the influence of music is one of the newest phases of musical therapy. It is an innovation having no limits. Truly, it is an aspect of the magic arts of the future.

To the average person the idea of music influencing vegetation seems incredible at first. It must be remembered, however, that the plant kingdom comes under the guidance of the angelic kingdom, and that Angels literally live, móve and have their being in music. By virtue of the intimate relationship between these two kingdoms, the magic power of harmony that exists in the higher extends to some degree into the life processes of the closely allied younger realm.

We know that in all religious communities throughout the world, and in all civilizations past and present, men have believed not only in the efficacy of silent prayer but in the power of sounds and ideas. It has ever been maintained that utterances of a spiritual name were the most penetrating, the most dynamic; but that all other types of sound and every idea had power in proportion to their nearness to truth and to God, and in relation to the world wherein they functioned. It was not assumed that the loudest noises were the mightiest; on the contrary, inaudible sounds like the "still, small voice" heard by Job were ofttimes of supreme potency. So also the keynotes of the planets in their orbits which the astronomer Kepler told of hearing are in fact the foundation music of the cosmos; though truly "whilst this muddy vesture of decay doth grossly close it in we cannot hear it."

The materialism of modern science is neither so

entrenched nor so formidable as it is popularly supposed to be. Leading universities are looking with favor upon experiments relative to the effect of sound, color and light upon human beings, animals and plants. The work of Dr. J. B. Rhine at Duke University is familiar to many. Researchers in other schools and universities are following Dr. Rhine's lead.

We may have to look to India for the most significant results of such experiments, for in that country the scientists have not the prejudices rife in the West to hamper their efforts. Mention has already been made of Dr. Bose, one of India's earliest pioneers. One of his published works on the subject is *Life Movements in Plants*. The research he initiated is being carried on at the same university under the direction of Dr. T. C. N. Singh, while a number of scientists in our own agricultural colleges are working along the same lines. Dr. Singh has shown that when plants are excited by single musical notes keyed to a high frequency, they give distinct responses; and that under musical irradiation certain plants have improved both in yield and quality.

Esotericists have long taught that there is a basic keynote for each kingdom in nature. These, taken collectively, form a chord, or diapason, of the planet earth itself.

In regard to the effect of prayer on plants, Dr. Singh has written that active work carried on since 1952, under strict laboratory conditions at the Annamalai University, has shown clearly that prayer does enhance the growth and well being of plants. The specimens used for this experiment were faithfully treated each day with prayer and then checked regularly against control plants. No audible mantra were used. The projection was mental and therefore silent, yet remarkable superiority in both vegetative activity and reproductiveness was noted. When two of the experimental plants suffered an attack of fungus, special healing prayers were used. This treatment not only cured the disease but enabled the patients to grow and flower more vigorously than the others, although the same material conditions were maintained in both groups.

In a comment upon these experiments it was pointed out that cell walls are very thin, and that protoplasm in its fluid state is most active in the growing region of the plant. Further, it is known that protoplasm is very highly irritable to such physical factors as light, temperature, humidity, wind, etc. But it was not known until after these experiments that it is sensitive to noise as well. The Indian commentators concluded that the prayers, in the form of thought waves, impinged upon and modified the protoplasm of the cells in the growing area of the plants.

As opposed to the foregoing, the Indian scientists mentioned another experiment with bacteria in petri-dish cultures. One dish was reserved as control; the others were cursed every day by chants. The bacteria which were cursed not only ceased to multiply but by the end of the experiment they were dead.

While India may be in the lead in this type of music experimentation, the West has its notable contributors, one being Dr. Rhine already cited. Another is Dr. Franklin Lohr of Princeton, who for many years past has headed experiments performed by the Religious Research Foundation. Dr. Lohr has demonstrated beyond all doubt the efficacy of prayer in the life, growth and well being of plants. Working under strict controls, it has been shown conclusively that prayer-treated specimens excelled in every respect those left unattended.

Thus physical science stands today at the threshold of basic occultism. It has actually proved one fundamental tenet of occult science: that man's thought forces are responsible for the creation and multiplication of harmful bacteria, and that the diseases of man are a literal out-picturing of his own evil thoughts and emotions. This has long been maintained by occultists.

Recently there appeared in the English magazine *Prediction* an interesting article, *Tone Your Plants to Music,* by the well-known writer-musician, Cyril Scott, who writes on various phases of esoteric music. Mr. Scott says in the beginning of his article that the Initiate known to students of occult science as the Master D. K. has stated: "By the discovery of the note of the vegetable kingdom, by its conjunction with others of nature's notes, and by its due sounding forth in different keys and combinations, will come the possibility to produce marvelous results within that kingdom, and to stimulate the activities of those devas who work wih flowers, fruits, trees and herbs."

Mr. Scott then comments: "The devas, I may perhaps remind some of my readers, is the generic term for the nature spirits ranging from the smallest fairies to those beings of great size and beauty which in the Christian religion are called angels.

"Even trees will yield to the power of love. One hot summer we rescued, from a demolition squad, a six-foot tree and transported it into our garden. It was in full leaf at the time, and gardening experts told us that being transplanted at the wrong time of year it could not possibly live.

"Nevertheless, having planted it, we suffused it with love for several minutes at intervals for a few days, and not only has it lived as a fine healthy tree, but it did not lose any of its leaves till the time when all except evergreens go bare."

Mr. Scott ends his admirable little treatise: "It may be that a few of my readers would like to try the music treatment on their house plants and then note the result. Recorded music in the key of F, the predominating nature-note for this planet (and also the note corresponding to the color green), would be the mood suitable for the purpose. Some who possess gardens may also wish to try this on flowerbeds.

"I grant that to the so-called 'man in the street,' the idea of 'entertaining' flowers with melody and harmony may seem a very curious one. But is it really so curious when we consider that we are now in the Aquarian Age, which is and will become more and more the age of unification in its widest sense? This will create a different attitude towards many things.

"Whereas in the recently ended Piscean Age none save occultists would have imagined any possible connection between flowers and the art of music, now, as the new age advances, this hitherto unsuspected fact will be increasingly recognized; and, moreover, to the advantage of mankind."

Chapter IX

MODERN MUSIC: ITS SCOPE AND MESSAGE

God has left for us an eternal memorial of Himself, our music which is the living God in our bosoms. Hence, we will preserve our music and ward off from it all sacrilegious hands, for if we hearken to frivolous and insincere music, we extinguish the last light God has left burning within us to lead the way to find Him anew.—*Richard Wagner*

As the attuning of music arouses emotions in the body to an unusual degree, well that there be choices made regarding what emotions are aroused and by what character of music. For there is a way that seemeth right to a man, but the end thereof taketh hold upon hell. As to the experiences that arise from music, choose that which is constructive in the experience and know it must partake of that which brings peace to the soul and not the gratifying of body — or of the emotion of the body only.
—*Edgar Cayce*

BY THE BEGINNING of the fifteenth century a wave of materialism began to engulf humanity. It increased in intensity and extent with each succeeding century, until today some liberal churchmen even disparage teachings about angelic Beings, considering them to be mere figments of the imagination. Information relative to Initiation has been banished from the Church at large. The sacred flame that should burn in the Holy of Holies has been virtually extinguished. Present world conditions are a fair index of the widespread negation of spiritual and moral culture. And men, having lost their soul light, compose music that has little or no soul power. To be popular it must be brilliant, exotic, diverting. Many people no longer turn to music for its spiritual benediction. Instead, it is merely a means of entertainment. So an era of modern music has been born.

In Part I of this volume we have endeavored to show that the music of any race or nation is a fair index of its physical, mental and spiritual evolvement. A recent *Art Review* stated that in the Golden Age of Greece the aspiration of an artist was to reproduce the human form in all its perfection of beauty and symmetrical proportions. The *Review* goes on to state that the work of a modern painter is to describe the stress and strain that a discordant and confused world has placed upon the bodies of the masses. This statement applies to modern music as much as it does to modern painting. In fact, it is an altogether adequate description of most music being produced at the present time.

To repeat, upon our Fifth Root Race was bestowed that most precious gift of all gifts, *mind*. Since its acquisition the work of evolutionary processes has been to spiritualize that mind. It is very evident that this has not yet been accomplished by the masses. St. Paul admonished: "Let this mind be in you, which was also in Christ Jesus." Had the human race reached this attainment, the Fatherhood of God and the brotherhood of man would have become a reality because the Golden Rule would prevail. On the contrary, the world today is an armed camp. Nations look upon one another with suspicion and every man's hand is against his brother. Hatred, fear, war and rumors of war are rampant — a condition that has set its impress upon music by producing a style characterized by dissonances and inharmonious intonations.

MUSIC OF CHALLENGE AND SEARCH

Popular music is teeming with unfulfilled desires and a longing to break through the veil that shrouds the Temple and stand in the Light Eternal. These yearnings being as yet unsatisfied, they have not yet reached their full and free expression in the music of this period. Rather, it retrogrades, exhausted from battling against darkness. Hence, modern music leaves the hearer dissatisfied, as though waiting for something to which it aspires but does not reach.

The Unanswered Question by Charles Ives is an outstanding example of this type of music. The strings and flutes beat in futility against empty space, vainly seeking the answer to this soul hunger, but that answer can be found only in regenerated man himself. Much of our modern music may well be termed a glorification of dissonances. Previous mention has been made of the fact that the early Church Fathers considered certain musical dissonances to be "devil music," which gives a clue to the sinister influence upon teen-agers of jazz that is so largely composed of dissonances.

Some writers claim that modern music was born in 1913 with Stravinsky's *Rite of Spring*, first performed in Paris. To both Stravinsky and Schoenberg has been allotted the distinction of being the father of modern music. Each of them has created many strange and bizarre combinations out of the conventional scale, while the latter has produced his own twelve-tone scale. These two modern composers make extravagant use of dissonances, wherein a materialistic mind loses touch completely with knowledge possessed by early religious musicians as to the sinister influence of dissonances.

Stravinsky and Schoenberg stand upon the threshold of the New Age and their music seems to be groping blindly for an answer to the meaning and purpose of life. But the answer they seek has not yet been found, so their music leaves the listener restless and oftentimes filled with a sense of profound disillusionment. Gifted though they are they have not been able to pass the thin veil that divides the seen from the unseen, the real from the unreal; but Schoenberg came close to parting this veil in his *Transfiguration*.

Stravinsky's work probably reached its climax in his *Symphony of the Psalms*. It is here that he seems to have touched that higher Something for which he appeared to have been searching in all of his other works. This composition, written to commemorate the fiftieth anniversary of the Boston Philharmonic Orchestra, is divided into three parts, the first of which is centered in the thirty-third Psalm, and is a prayer for protection and succor. The second part is centered in the thirty-ninth Psalm and is a prayer of thanksgiving for having touched the Light. The third part is concerned with the hundred and fiftieth Psalm and from beginning to end is a great allelujah in glorification of the high spiritual attainment portrayed by this Psalm.

One modern composer who has made the ascent and been able to bring much of the magic and power of celestial music to his compositions is Claude Debussy. He has beautifully demonstrated it in his score for the operatic version of Maeterlinck's *Pelleas and Melisande*. The music is so tenuous, so mystically beautiful, that a listener is often caught up in the ecstasy of some strange exhilaration and at other times is brought to the very verge of tears.

As mentioned elsewhere in this volume, every activity of nature has its own musical accompaniment. It is only when one has eyes to see and ears to hear that he begins to apprehend something of nature's majestic laws and their harmonious working. Only then does he understand that "Nature is God in manifestation."

In the music of *Pelleas and Melisande* Debussy describes a mist rising from the sea. For this passage he uses the keynote of invisible nature spirits that are attuned to the sea and perform their activities in the watery element. Again, he uses dissonances to describe dark, inimical forces that lurk in the cavern wherein Pelleas and Melisande search for her lost wedding ring. Then there is an exquisitely tremulous song of death as the gentle spirit of Melisande breaks its fragile earthly bond and ascends into higher, happier realms. Death is always accompanied by its own music, but only the musician who can listen between inner and outer spheres, and whose sensitivity enables him to record the heavenly song, can transcribe it for human hearing.

The score of *Pelleas and Melisande* is music belonging to the New Age. It heralds that which is to be; that which will lift man from the earthly to the celestial, from the mortal to the immortal. There will come about a gradual transferrence of values from the terrestrial world wherein they are now centered to the divine archetypal world. Debussy has done so in the score of *Pelleas and Melisande* in which he has given mankind true metaphysical music.

JAZZ — ITS ORIGIN AND INFLUENCE IN THE MODERN WORLD

We repeat that the darkly suggestive rhythms of jazz were used by the Great Ones in prehistoric Lemuria to arouse man's desire nature, which then needed quickening. This served the processes of development at that stage of human evolution. It is different now. In the present stage of development, the emotional nature needs to be calmed down and controlled. But jazz acts to the contrary. It excites the emotions and plays up the desires. And most devotees of jazz are teen-agers upon whom it has an especially deleterious effect. From the age of fourteen to twenty-one the adolescent goes through a crucial time in the formation of character as well as of body. During these years the desire body is in the process of development while the mind has not yet reached a point where it can control the emotions. To be continually exposed to jazz, which over-stimulates the emotional nature, can have but the one effect of being destructive if not actually disastrous.

The result of this condition is seen on all sides: in the use of drugs and alcohol by young people; in the frantic love of speed on the highways, which gives a false sense of freedom to the excitable youngsters; robberies, rape, and even murder committed by some who are so young as to be scarcely adolescent. Jazz and juvenile delinquency are twins. Where one flourishes the other will appear. And those who assist in the dissemination of these destructive rhythms are drawing upon themselves a harvest of sorrow and pain, though they may be entirely ignorant of any wrong-doing; for ignorance of the law excuses no one. "Though the mills of God grind slowly, yet they grind exceedingly small."

The psychic conditions created in times of war lay humanity open to the most damaging onslaughts of the Dark Forces, for at such times it is as if the human psyche is stripped of its protective sheath of high-mindedness and idealism and is responsive to evil impulses, which it accepts as its own. The legacy of World War I was jazz, which can be traced to African sources. It came from Africa with the slave trade of colonial times and took root in America, undergoing an evolution in its new home, and then bursting into blossom after the first world war. Its current popularity originated in the night clubs of New Orleans. From New Orleans it spread through the nation, found a welcome in Paris night clubs, and from Paris infected all of Europe and finally the world.

Consonances and Dissonances

No less an authority on music than Dr. Howard Hanson, Director of the Rochester Eastman School of Music, interested himself in the study of music as a healing agent. Some of Dr. Hanson's conclusions were interestingly detailed in the *American Journal of Psychiatry*. We quote:

"A pleasing vitamin in music is consonance. When composers wish to ennoble, invigorate and inspire their listeners, they depend heavily upon consonances. An upsetting virus in music is dissonance, a combination of sounds full of sonorous tension which may produce anything from vague impatience to acute aural distress. When composers wish to disturb their listeners, make them weep, sigh, or foam at the mouth, they do it with dissonances.

"Practically all music of Western civilization," this noted musician continues, "consists of consonances variously interspersed with dissonances. However, throughout musical history the dissonances have shown a tendency to crowd the consonances out. Palestrina, who composed the greatest of all Catholic liturgical music, expressed himself almost entirely in consonances. Johann Sebastian Bach, a product of the more individualistic Protestant Reformation, used dissonances liberally, especially in his impassioned and emotional moments."

So also did the great master of musical drama, Richard Wagner. An example of his liberal use of consonances is to be noted in the Prelude to *Lohengrin;* and his even more liberal use of dissonances, in the Bacchanale of *Tannhauser.*

Spiritual scientists understand that there are two great streams of musical force being released on this planet by invisible Hierarchies. The consonances represent the constructive force; the dissonances, the destructive force. The former is used by the Angels and the latter by the Lucifers, the fallen Angels. With the increase in materialistic thinking since the Middle Ages the tendency has been, as noted by Dr. Hanson, toward an augmented use of dissonances — the consonances strengthening man's higher nature; the dissonances strengthening his desire nature. The work of Angels is to bind together, to lift up, to harmonize; the work of Lucifers is to separate, to pull down, to rend asunder. The signature of the Angels is harmony; that of the Lucifers is discord.

In view of the above, Dr. Hanson's closing words are most significant. Saying he is worried about the widespread use of dissonances in jazz, he adds: "I hesitate to think of what the effect of music upon the next generation will be if the present school of hot jazz continues to develop unabated. It should provide an increasing number of patients for psychiatric hospitals, and it is therefore only poetic justice that musical therapeutics should develop at least to the point where music serves as an antidote for itself."

In the earlier part of this volume we have aimed to show how the fine arts of any civilization reflect the spiritual condition of their particular time. This is emphatically shown in the architecture, sculpture, painting and music of our present age.

During the medieval centuries the fine arts were all considered to be spiritual messengers to mankind from God, their inspiration deriving from celestial sources. With the beginning of the fifteenth century a change of attitude became manifest, as spiritual interests were superseded by the material. Since then materiality has increased to such an extent that in the present century virtually half of the world has become blatantly atheistic. In the so-called Christian countries religion has become largely institutionalized and Churchianity has to a great extent taken the place of Christianity.

Many young people today appear to be immune to religious interests. A professor of science in one of our leading universities recently observed that among ten thousand science students only fifty gave any evidence of interest in spiritual matters. The younger generation, particularly those who are studying in the larger universities, in this country, are rapidly discarding the Bible as an out-moded and superstitious book and are replacing it with the facts of material science.

This may seem to be of little importance, but the life that is centered in God or All-Good possesses an inner feeling of security, peace and well-being which all the inharmonies and confusions of the outer world can never take away. It is truly that great peace which passeth understanding of which the Bible sings. It was the beauty of this incomparable inner peace which was the supreme message of the fine arts during the Middle Ages, and as man has turned away from this inner light so the fine arts have ceased to give forth the message of peace, harmony and beauty. This is especially notable in the abstractions of modern painting and sculpture, in the lack of coherence and continuity in contemporary poetry, and in the dissonances and inharmonies in current music; all of which are remarkably evidenced in the opera *Wozzeck,* by Alban Berg, a work of stark tragedy from beginning to end. None of the characters in this opera evince the slightest humanitarian feeling toward one another, not even the children. Each is absorbed in his own selfish interests, utterly indifferent to the weal or woe of those about him. The opera opens on tragedy and ends on double tragedy with a note of bitter irony. The keynote of the opera sounds the theme of sinister doom, obvious and inevitable from the outset. There is nothing elevating or inspiring either in the story or the music, and it is evident that this is intentional. And so the music is truly expressive of the motives and stresses dominant in the discordant and half-godless world of today. Like much twentieth-century music, *Wozzeck* expresses confusion of mind, darkness, turmoil, restless seeking and searching for something that is never found in the places where it is sought.

The message of the higher arts in this modern day are well described in the words of the poet:

> Voices crying in the night,
> Voices crying for the light—
> And with no language but a cry.

Chapter X

NEW AGE MUSIC

THE EVOLUTION OF MUSIC PARALLELS THE EVOLUTION OF MAN

Love is the keynote, Joy is the music, Power is the strain, Knowledge is the performer, The infinite All is the composer and audience.

We know only the preliminary discords which are as fierce as the harmony shall be great; but we shall arrive surely at the fugue of the divine Beatitudes.—*Sri Aurobindo*

Oh music! Thou who bringest the receding waves of eternity nearer to the weary heart of man as he stands upon the shores and longs to cross over! Art thou the evening breeze of life, or the morning air of the future one?—*Jean Paul*

IN THE APPROACHING New Age art and science will take their place beside religion as equal media for the expression of the triune spirit of man. They will no longer be set apart as at present, when religion is looked upon as sacred; art and science, as secular. This arbitrary distinction has grown up during the course of our material civilization and will, therefore, pass with it.

In the New Age people everywhere will enter into a realization of their human solidarity. *Unity* will be their keyword, and racial consciousness will be furthered by music. Musicians will be inspired to make unity the central theme of their compositions. This will be particularly noticeable in national anthems that will be not only national but international.

It is upon the patriotic folk songs of a people that the signature of the Race Spirit is impressed. They capture the very soul of a people and impart to it added life and vigor. Well was it said that anyone who had ever heard the French singing the *Marseillaise* will never doubt that the nation will someday be renewed in splendor. A national anthem is infused with ideals, aspirations and hopes whereby a nation can move securely and rapidly in the direction of its own destiny. By frequent repetition it welds a people into unity of thought and purpose; hence, its constant use in such crises as war and disaster, when solidarity of action backed by faith and hope becomes all-important. In the power of music, nationalism will gradually merge into internationalism. Harbingers of this merging are Ernest Bloch and Ludwig von Beethoven.

We have endeavored to show that through the ages the evolution of music has kept pace with the evolution of man. It will necessarily continue to be so in the future. This being true, a knowledge of future evolutionary trends will indicate new developments in musical expression. Such a trend is found in the late Ernest Bloch's rhapsody, *America,* a composition which sounds forth the dream of universal brotherhood and portrays the eventual triumph of idealism.

Ideals for future realization also found musical expression in the inspired works of Beethoven. Perhaps his two greatest are the *Missa Solemnis* and the *Ninth Symphony,* both of which call the world to peace and human brotherhood. To forward the realization of these hopes was the aim and purpose of this great composer's life and work. The last movement of his *Ninth Symphony,* with its divine *Ode to Joy,* proclaims the fruition of the ideals he served with such majestic power as to literally open the heavens and make audible the proclamation of the Christ: "Behold, I make all things new."

The three most important events in human life are birth, marriage and death. Now, due to man's ignorance regarding the verities of existence, it is marriage only that is celebrated with music. In the New Age, however, a spirit will be ushered into physical expression upon the wings of melody; and when its earthly stay is ended, it will be to strains of music that the spirit will gain its final release.

MUSIC'S SUPREME MISSION

If the mind and the body are to be well you must begin by curing the soul.—*Plato*

Music originated in the efforts of nascent humanity to reproduce the sounds of nature: harmony, melody and rhythm. In their early development human beings were both clairvoyant and clairaudient. They could hear the keynote of the wind, of the beating surf, of a crashing storm. Their first chants were composed of a mingling of these varied tones — chants later transcribed in their folk songs.

The latest findings of material science are arriving at the same conclusions as those of primitive man. There is a scientific statement to the effect that *this earth is a vast harmonic wave system which is built and sustained by unheard music*. All great musical composers have been connected, consciously or unconsciously, with this source of music — a fact which enabled them to become masters of their art. Their compositions contain specific messages brought through from high realms for the definite purpose of bettering world conditions and bestowing upon mankind greater illumination.

The works of Bach play directly upon man's mind to stimulate his mental faculties and quicken his spiritual processes. Haydn produced miracle music that opens doors to angelic communication. Debussy's productions build a bridge between the actual and the ideal. Ravel's invite a hearer into fairyland. Schubert and Schumann iterate a message from transcendental realms. To anyone writing or teaching along musical lines, the works of these two composers offer assistance and inspiration. Sibelius and Grieg are both music-poets. They describe not only the outer beauties of nature, but marvels of hidden revelations unseen and unheard by the average person.

The author once wrote in an article titled *Rhapsody of Spring*: "We noted a wild peach tree adorned with pink-and-white blossoms. As Angels blessed each tiny worker its robes assumed tones of pink and white and it went unerringly to poise itself upon a flower petal bearing its own distinctive hue.

"The motion and movements of both Angels and nature spirits are in complete accord with the glorious symphony of nature that becomes clearer and more powerful as the season advances. Finally the etheric pattern for all the plant kingdom is complete. Its forces then merge into and unite with the outer physical form of tree and vine. Not until this occurs does man become aware of the miracle of spring. It is this amazing revelation of the inner working of nature that is brought to the soul of mankind through the music of Sibelius and Grieg."

The music of Mendelssohn touches the very soul of beauty. It is filled with that high truth of which Keats sings when he asserts, "Beauty is truth, truth beauty." Cesar Franck brings a fragrant benediction that plays upon man's devotional soul. This is particularly true of his organ music. Compositions of Scriabin should be a revelation to those working with the inner forces of sound and color. Smetana, the Czech composer, is a true New Age musician. He envisions a glorious day when there shall be no barrier between man and man, nation and nation. Verdi reveals that he is a great lover of his kind. His music not only invites to romance but it envisions the glory of the brotherhood of man. Mozart's music will, in the coming years, be used in connection with discoveries relative to the subconscious mind.

Richard Wagner composed true initiatory music, written for the purpose of awakening certain centers latent in the body of man. These centers, when fully functioning, will lift the human race far beyond our present concepts. Wagner's *Parsifal* treats of the Christ Mystery. For this reason, Wagner wished that *Parsifal* would never be presented outside of Beyreuth. He desired each performance to be a veritable initiatory experience, and hoped that every person witnessing a performance had made a spiritual pilgrimage to his theatre for this express purpose. However, his wish that the sacred character of this music-drama be safeguarded by confining its performances exclusively to his Temple of Music in Beyreuth did not long remain in effect. Even at the risk of its performances being tainted by the prevailing secularism, the demand of music lovers that this consecrational music-drama be made accessible to a much wider audience than would be possible by its retention at Beyreuth alone, seemed to justify over-riding the composer's wish in the matter.

Truly, Wagner was a musical prophet who lived before

his day. In the New Age now dawning music will again be a ritual of Initiation, and Wagner's music will come into its own.

As we have stated frequently, Beethoven's is cosmic music. His is truly "space music." In the years to come, as man ventures farther and farther into space to discover the myriad wonders to be found therein, an entirely new evaluation and a deeper, more profound appreciation will be awarded to the sublime music and the high mission of this great and noble soul. The magical power of Ludwig von Beethoven's music, together with his lofty inspiration, have set their impress upon this earth planet for all time.

To resurrect humanity from the limiting conditions into which it has fallen is the true mission of music, for it has power to restore man to his all-but-forgotten divine estate. It has been one of the principal factors operating in Western nations to save the human spirit from succumbing completely to the benumbing effects of a materialized and mechanized civilization.

It may here be added that evidences we find in the arts and elsewhere of a decline in virtues of the heart do not necessarily mean retrogression. Humanity ever continues to develop such virtues to a higher degree of expression, but historic and evolutionary progression is never in a straight line. The ascent follows a cyclic movement of ebb and flow. When we discover the falling off of a certain unfoldment it may be we are witnessing simply the slack that follows and precedes the stress by which we mount ever upward on the spiral of growth.

HARMONY, MELODY AND RHYTHM:

Their Significance in the Life of Evolving Mankind

Alan Hovhaness, an American composer of Armenian birth, writes interestingly of the power of ancient music and of the resurrected power which will be found in music of the future: "Armenian music belongs to the ancient world when *ragas,* melody lines, and *talas,* rhythmic lines, were main pillars of universal music. When music was melody and rhythm, when each melodic combination was a gift of the gods, each rhythmic combination was a mantram to unlock a key of power in nature, then music was one of the mysteries of the elements, of the planetary systems, of the worlds, visible and invisible.

"The cycle of Western civilization since the Renaissance has developed outer laws of music and the outer forces of nature. This knowledge is limited. It pierces no veil and brings no well-being to the inner life—it offers no remedy for the disaster of inward disintegration — it leaves the human nucleus unthreaded, uncentered, unrevealed, with no hope of recovering the form or the central sun of existence.

"The laws of *raga* and *tala* bring about attunement with the inner forces of nature, freedom from the limitation of consciousness of life and death, indifference to the storm of broken threads. If it be the end of a cycle, it is nothing. There have been and will be far nobler cycles."

In his brochure Mr. Hovhaness deals with ancient music and the significance of melody and rhythm. These are but two of the three component parts of music. The third, which is harmony, is of a later development. In relation to man's threefold being, harmony is of the heart as melody is of the head and rhythm is of the limbs. Harmony develops as the heart quality comes into expression. It is of the spirit and is central to our very being. In an orchestra melody is carried by the wind instruments, harmony by the strings, rhythm by the percussion instruments. Violins, the principal carriers of harmony, found their place in orchestras later than did flutes and drums.

An interesting fact in connection with the above observations regarding strings came from an orchestra leader a few years ago when he decried the "conspicuous dearth of first class string players." Later, a two-column article appeared in the *New York Times* dealing with the decline in both the standard and the number of players of stringed instruments, and how this disconcerting trend could be reversed. The educational, artistic and economic factors involved were fully discussed. But as one might well expect, the underlying spiritual causation, always present though not always discernible, was not touched upon.

Reasons for this reported weakness in the string section of orchestras is not difficult to determine. When aggressive materialism makes such assaults on civilizations as it has in our time, the heart quality is forceably depressed. Again, when discord replaces concord on such a world-wide scale as it has, musically speaking, the strings suffer. These spiritual weaknesses have been reflected in a decline of those instruments in an orchestra which express the warm, harmonizing elements of human nature. Such a condition is not accidental. It does not happen without due cause. Every physical effect has a spiritual origin, could we but trace the connection.

Powers possessed by those who have attained to Mastership will eventually become common to the people at large. Initiates of Egypt's Golden Age foreshadowed this development in their thirteen-stringed lyre, the strings being attuned to the twelve spiritual centers and the ego of an illumined one.

THE HEALING POWER OF THE NEW AGE AQUARIAN MUSIC

In the Aquarian Age healing miracles will be performed by groups scientifically organized in harmony with the vibratory rhythms of the heavens. A circle of twelve healers, each one in attunement with one of the twelve zodiacal signs, could perform wonders. It is along such lines that the magic of "musical medicine" will come into its own. Application of such healing potencies will not be limited to man's mind and body, but will be an agency for building and healing his soul as well. Also, it will become a more and more prominent feature of rituals observed in Temples and Initiation. Specific rhythms will be utilized to stimulate vital currents of the head centers, thus aiding in the development of extended sight and hearing. Possessing these augmented faculties, a practitioner will be able to hear the "tones" of the several bodies of man and, if any of them are out of harmony, to prescribe corrective measures.

Still more powerful musical vibrations will aid in liberating an individual's spirit from his body, not by death but through Initiation, if the time is ripe for such development. As he gains in ability to work consciously either in or out of his body, man will become more and more cognizant of his immortality here and now.

A certain type of Temple music will be used to facilitate the clearance of karma and the recovery of memory regarding past lives. This activity will be keyed to the musical note of the heart. Truly it is written: "Music is the mysterious key of memory, unlocking the hoarded treasures of the heart." And again, in the words of Edward Bulwer Lytton: "Tones, at times, in music, will bring back forgotten things."

The rhythm of the human heart is attuned to the keynote of the indwelling spirit. The more soulful a person becomes, the more rhythmic is his heart action. Consequently, the materialistic thinking of our present civilization has brought with it a heavy harvest of heart afflictions. The initial note of the incarnated ego centers in the heart and finds its echoes in the pulsings of the blood, in the currents of the nervous systems, and in the circulatory and fluidic functions of the body. The human body is an orchestra, each organ an instrument, complete within itself. Herein is to be found the basis for musical therapy. In the New Age music will be the most important and successful of all therapeutic methods.

The highest mission of music is to serve as a link between God and man. It builds a bridge over which angelic and fairy hosts can come closer to humankind. New Age music will erect firmer structures for such communion than have been possible in the past. Debussy and Ravel have produced compositions especially designed to serve this purpose. The grandest music of the present age was written out of the Christian impulse to voice the love that binds the heart of man to the heart of God. Music of this latter type will reach new heights in time to come. Then love will encompass the earth and the brotherhood of man will be realized in truth and in deed.

Popular music of today is keyed primarily to the sense life, while in lyric notes of melody the soul finds expression. Harmony is the keynote of the spirit. It was to initiatory harmonies that St. Cecelia, patron saint of music, referred when, unsatisfied with earthly music, she cried out, "Oh, that I might but hear the song of praise that those Holy Three sang in the glowing flames of Creation's Song."

OUTSTANDING EXPONENTS OF NEW AGE AQAURIAN MUSIC

Choral music is a communal activity. Solos serve to further individualization. Hence, as a community life grows stronger choral singing will increase. It will be a natural and spontaneous outpouring of group experience and effort.

An augmented musical scale will be another New Age development. We are now familiar with the pentatonic (five tone), the septatonic (seven tone) and the chromatic (twelve tone and half-tone) scales. As future unfoldment will increase the range of human hearing, additional tones will be employed to meet expanding musical needs. Scriabin and Debussy are pioneers in this field.

In his fascinating book on music, Cyril Scott states that the Russian composer Scriabin is a bridge-builder connecting the angelic with the human world. There is no doubt but that rapture of vision and exhilaration of soul were his during the inner-plane journeys he has described in his beautiful *Poem of Ecstasy*. This composer was a true exponent of New Age music. At the time of his death in 1915, at the early age of forty-four, he was working on what he hoped would be his masterpiece: a composition correlating music with color. A portion of the work was to be performed by orchestra and chorus. Then the same part was to be thrown upon a screen as a symphony in color. In this manner music and color were to alternate throughout the entire composition. To this combination Scriabin planned to release at various intervals rare and exotic fragrances. It is evident he was reviewing some of the ancient Mystery Temple rites wherein music, color and scent were combined for the purpose of developing certain types of ecstatic vision.

Scriabin looked upon members of his audience as "experimental initiates." By thus lifting their consciousness he hoped they might contact higher spiritual realms, learn something of the reality and permanence of them and, by means of exalted vision, bring back something of the glories there to be found. He was also working upon a composition which, he expected, would loosen the bond that links an- ego to its physical encasement, thereby making it possible for it to take soul flights—or, as the Masonic Fraternity designates such "wages of the Master," to "travel in foreign countries." Another of Scriabin's ventures was an attempt to create music that would easily sever the bond between spirit and its body at the time of the transition called death.

Scriabin was a true messenger and prophet of the Aquarian Age. He was rediscovering the latent powers and magic of music, color and perfume, knowledge lost with the passing of ancient Mystery Temples but to be put to use again even more effectually during the coming age. It is significant to note that long years after Scriabin's death the motion picture producers are experimenting with the release of varying fragrances appropriate to scenes being enacted. It will be interesting to watch the transplanting of this revived art to popular entertainment and educational media. Certain it is that with Scriabin's demise there passed from this plane one of music's highly inspired exponents.

The New Age will not only uncover a new octave in music but also a new and higher octave in color. Nicholas Roerich, possibly the most famous of modern painters, has given an intimation of this in some of the magnificent canvasses whereon he depicts varying degrees of initiatory attainment.

In *Science and Music,* the late Sir James Jeans observes that a "fifty-three note scale would give far purer harmonies than the present scale and we can imagine some future ages finding it worthy of adoption in spite of its added complexities, especially if mechanical devices replace human fingers in the performances of music . . . If ever music becomes independent of the human hand," he writes further, "may not the race then elect to use a continuous scale in which every interval can be made perfect?"

Given in this volume is a quotation from Mozart wherein he refers to the wonders of the music of the future. He mentions a higher and wider scale which will introduce many sounds the human ear is now incapable of hearing. Among these new sounds will be the glorious music of angelic chorales. As men hear these they will cease to consider Angels as mere "figments of the imagination." Their music will uplift, inspire and heal. Then it will be understood whence Richard Wagner received his inspiration for the Holy Grail motif he used in *Lohengrin* and *Parsifal.* They are direct transcriptions from angelic choirs.

Going still higher, one will be able to catch the great songs of praise and rejoicing sent forth by vast assemblages of celestial Beings in rank above rank and sphere above sphere, such as those which witnessed the coronation of the Blessed Virgin. It is then that an inspired one will realize the origin of the magnificent chorale with which Beethoven concluded his *Ninth Symphony,* for this is also a transcription of the music of heavenly choirs.

Much is heard today about space travel. In the New Age man will not only have ability to travel amid the stars, but he will be able to hear their sublime music. Each and every star possesses its individual keynote; and this mass harmony of cosmic music will be an inspiration to great composers of that era. Richard Wagner introduces a strain of this music in the final scene of his dramatic *Ring Cycle.* To this strain of unearthly sweetness. Wotan listens as he watches the destruction of things-as-they-are while across the rainbow bridge he sees the beauties of a day-that-is-to-be.

The keynote of New Age music is *transmutation.* It plays its part in carrying foward nature's evolutionary processes in gradually transforming the old order into new and nobler forms.

As previously stated, Beethoven and Wagner were both musical prophets. They belonged to no specific time or race; the message they gave is universal and their music immortal. Beethoven's mission was to bring down fragments of pure cosmic music. His is truly Music of the Spheres, the echoing of planetary harmonies. Only when man will have learned to travel through interplanetary space will he comprehend the magnificence of this great composer's music.

Wagner's music sounds the keynote of the Mysteries. It was his mission to reawaken mankind to the reality and importance of the Mystery Schools. This knowledge was temporarily lost under the wave of materialism which has engulfed the modern world. Wagner musically proclaims the glories of the Mysteries and points a way whereby men may one day be emancipated by their light.

The horizon widens as the New Age draws nearer. It is beckoning us onward and upward. It holds a glorious promise of a radiant future that awaits us. We are still a "little lower than the angels" and "it doth not yet appear what we shall become."